ONE HIT WONDER

A SAMANTHA TRUE NOVEL

KRISTI ROSE

Vintage Housewife Books

PO BOX 842

Ridgefield, Wa 98642

www.kristirose.net

Publisher's Note: This is a work of fiction. Names, characters, places, and incidents are a product of the author's imagination. Locales and public names are sometimes used for atmospheric purposes. Any resemblance to actual people, living or dead, or to businesses, companies, events, institutions, or locales is completely coincidental.

Cover Design © 2019 Strong Image Editing

Edited by: CDM Editing

ONE HIT WONDER/ Kristi Rose. *-- 1st edition*

❀ Created with Vellum

The Girl He Loves

ONE HIT WONDER

A SAMANTHA TRUE NOVEL

Put up or shut up

A year into Samantha True's forensic photography classes she knows three things:

1. Crime scenes are messy.
2. Especially when you throw up on them.
3. She may not be cut out for this.

When the police drag her to an investigation, she's just as baffled by the scene. With clues like superhero masks, disco balls, and Bigfoot, are they ever going to find who did it?

As she digs deeper into the photographic evidence, she realizes her small town is full of secrets. And she might be happier staying in the dark.

One Hit Wonder is the Prequel to Samantha True Mystery Series.

KRISTI ROSE

ONE HIT
WONDER

CHAPTER ONE

W hen a person ignored opportunity's knock, was their life changed for the worse? This question often weighed on my mind. Would I regret not answering the call? The go-getter in me said, "Samantha, you got this." The part of me that hated the go-getter said, "Screw that! Ignore everyone and go back to sleep."

In my case, opportunity knocked around four in the morning when I was in bed fighting the Godforsaken flu. Opportunity's timing sucked.

Yet, when the phone gave its third ring, I picked it up.

"Be at River Forest Road ASAP," the county dispatcher had said. "Car versus deer, no deceased on the scene except the deer. You're getting pics for the insurance company." Clearly annoyed, she continued, "The accident occurred between town and the water tower, whatever that means. That's the best I have for directions."

"I know where that is," I'd croaked, my throat parched. Day two of the flu, and the virus was the clear winner.

I lived fourteen minutes away from said water tower and smack in the middle of the town she'd been referring to, Wind River. Our city was too small to support twenty-four-hour emergency services. After nine p.m., all calls were handled by the larger cities in our county.

The dispatcher sighed. "Oh, one more thing. Boyd Bartell won't be there. Apparently, he's had too much to drink at his brother's wedding. You'll be supervised by the cops on the scene. They'll tell you what to do. Good luck, intern."

"Okay, thanks," I said, my head still on the pillow, my eyes still closed. She disconnected the call, but I kept the phone to my ear, slow to make any move. Where would I find the energy to get out of bed?

For the last six weeks, I'd been waiting to get this call. Part of obtaining a forensic photography degree and graduating college was getting this fieldwork experience. Here was the chance to prove I could do the job. Being feverish and one degree shy of a hallucination was just my luck.

I slid from the bed onto the floor. Over my tank top, I threw on my favorite Seahawks sweatshirt procured from half under my bed and decided my yoga pants would have to do. While I waited for my Keurig to brew me a cup of coffee, I stuffed my feet into sneakers and chugged back a dose of flu meds. Then I pulled my hair into a loose ponytail. My head was already pounding.

With my camera bag over my shoulder and coffee in hand, I shuffled to LC, my classic wagoner. LC was named after the explorers Lewis and Clark. Like the explorers, my vehicle enjoyed being off-road and was temperamental.

I pointed LC in the direction of River Forest Road. While pit-staining my Seahawks sweatshirt waiting for the flu meds to kick in, I made a silent prayer for good luck to help me pull this off.

Though I wanted to be a forensic photographer, I worried about the profession being a good fit. Not because I couldn't capture the images needed since photography had long stopped being my passion and had become my default, a way to conceal my shortcoming. Though my brain struggled to make sense of symbols like letters and words, it did an

3

amazing job of capturing images and storing them long-term in the finest of details. A dyslexic photographer with a photographic memory. Life could be cruel.

Many of the images they'd shown in class were gruesome. When you see bad things, you can't unsee them. Doubly so for me. These sorts of images changed how a person approached every day, because now you've learned the unimaginable is possible. Was I willing to straddle the line between dark and light every day? That was the question I'd been asking myself since this course began. As a backup plan, I'd started studying for my private investigator's license. A guest lecturer at school said being a PI was mostly following up on insurance claims. Easy peasy. Didn't sound too hard, or grotesque, and the lecturer said reading requirements were minimal.

The ride out to River Forest Road took me an extra seven minutes. I didn't trust myself to drive normal speed since keeping my focus on the road was difficult, and the coffee wasn't helping. Instead, the acrid taste was heavy on my tongue, and the drink was sitting like sludge in my belly.

My body convulsed from part shivers, part apprehension, and I blew out a breath to steady my nerves.

The flashing lights of the patrol car were a welcome sight, and I pulled LC behind it. Ahead was a torch-red Mustang Saleen, occasional thin tendrils of smoke coming from the engine. The car sat across both lanes, so no telling which direction he'd been headed.

"Holy crap," I said. That Mustang belonged to Kenny Greevey Junior and was maybe a week off the showroom floor.

The cops on the scene were circling the car. Junior was on the side of the road, looking distressed and sitting on his haunches with his hands over his head. He was dressed for work in a suit but jacket off.

I slid out of LC. Autumn was full swing in the Pacific Northwest, making the night cool. The chilled wind was refreshing against my hot skin. I desperately wanted to stretch out on the cold ground but forced myself to walk toward the scene.

On autopilot, I slung my camera across my body and flipped off the lens cap. I placed my unused crime scene kit on the hood of my Wagoneer.

The patrol car had its headlights on bright, and four portable floodlights were shining on the scene. I scoped out the cops handling the call. The night became even more craptastic at hyperdrive speed when one of the cops turned out to be Leo Stillman, a blight to society if there ever was one.

Oh, he was easy on the eyes. Strong Native American features with gray eyes and hair as dark as his soul. Everyone loved Leo. Everyone but me. He was Mr. Awesome. But I had another A word in mind when I thought of Leo.

He kept his hair short, which accentuated his angular facial features, like an all-seeing, all-knowing eagle primed to strike. A look he had replicated as an eagle tattoo on his forearm.

We'd gone to high school together. He, along with Junior, had graduated in my sister's class two years ahead of me. Leo had been the starting quarterback who'd received a full college ride, though it was known he had no desire to be a professional ball player. When he graduated, he returned to Wind River to serve on the Tribal Board for the Cowlitz Tribe and recently joined the local law enforcement agency. If I were feeling better, I'd razz him about being a rookie.

I don't know why he disliked me, but he did. And I believed not returning the hostility was inconsiderate, so I gave it everything I had.

I moved closer to the other cop, the one lieutenant on the force, Bruce Rawlings. Clearly the force matched personalities because in a butt-head contest, either of these guys could've taken it.

"Someone request a photographer?" I croaked and held up my camera.

Rawlings arched a brow and stepped toward me. "Intern, huh? Try not to goof it up."

"I suppose that part is up to you since you'll be telling me what to do. What do you need?" I closed my eyes in what was supposed to be a blink but turned into a second-long nap. I snapped back to attention.

Leo came to where we stood and surveyed me. His thumbs in his utility belt, he said, "You can't do this. You can barely stand." He held a finger up in front of my face. The finger wavered from side to side.

Or maybe that was me.

Yeah, he might have a point, but I wasn't about to let him know I agreed with him. I was gonna take these stupid pictures, then I was gonna go home and sleep on my cold bathroom floor.

Leo asked. "Are you drunk?"

Was he kidding? "No, I'm not drunk," I said with bite. "I have the flu and a temperature of one hundred and fifty-two billion."

"Are you sure? Seems to me you might be drunk. You're a mess." He scoffed. "Some professional. You shouldn't be here."

"Are you telling me to leave?" This opportunity was going south fast. I had two options. Bail now and hope to get another call. Not my favorite option, but far easier than sticking around where I wasn't wanted and my photos and performance would be judged harshly. Or, option two, make staying and completing the job Leo or Rawling's idea, thereby somewhat shifting the responsibility for my outcome to one of them. I mentally crossed my fingers for option two.

I waited for two beats then turned and walked toward LC.

From behind me he sighed. "Stop. We all want to go home. It's getting close to five. Take your pictures so we can leave."

I pivoted. "I'm shocked you haven't ripped this camera from me and taken the pictures yourself, since you're Mr. Skilled at everything. I bet you'll outrank Rawlings here any day."

Rawlings snickered. "She's got your number. Looks like she doesn't think you're such a stud, rookie. About time we met someone who doesn't swoon when they see you."

Leo scoffed. "The only thing Samantha has is—"

I leaned forward and hissed, "You gonna keep talking or tell me where you want me to start."

Leo pointed to the sports car. "Junior wrecked the car."

I glanced over my shoulder to Kenny Greevey Junior. "Is he okay?"

Junior was Mr. Wonderful, in the sincerest way. His kid brother Kevin was a hellion; even trouble was afraid to get caught with him. But Junior? Nope. Handsome, albeit more average than dreamboat, and not overly friendly to the point his actions were questionable. He was the cliché of a genuinely nice guy.

I whispered when I asked the unthinkable. "Is he drunk?"

Junior would never break a law. He'd been president of the student council in high school. He had loved rules then, and I couldn't imagine that fervor for compliance didn't carry into adulthood.

Rawlings said, "Nope. Knocked himself out when the deer hit the windshield. Sat out here for a while before he came to and called it in himself."

"Is he coming from work or going to it?" A suit at pre-dawn could mean one of two things. One heck of a night or one workaholic.

Leo crossed his arms. "Going to work."

Workaholic. "Poor guy," I said. "Is an ambulance on the way?"

"Poor deer." Leo nodded in the direction of

the car. "Why don't you go get pictures of everything. Particularly the deer and where the impact happened."

Rawlings said to me, "Junior said he didn't need one. His dad's coming to get him."

Hitting a deer on River Forest Road wasn't unheard of. One side of the road was a forest and the other the river. Hitting a deer required little more than poor timing and speeding on the straightaway. Perhaps Junior did have a wild streak and was "opening up" his new car. Irony would be wrecking the one time he decided to speed.

I circled to the front of the car and adjusted two of the floodlights to avoid glare, shadows, and to illuminate most of the car.

Once done, the view in front of me became clear and the contents of my stomach threatened to spew out. Only speed-gulping kept everything down. The contorted body of the deer was lying on top of the hood, half in the windshield, half out. The head on the hood, its dark, glassy eyes staring at me.

I pressed my lips together in hopes of retaining control. Leo came up behind me and pointed out shots he thought the insurance company would want.

"Get pictures of the body. And behind the car where there aren't skid marks."

I brought my camera up to my eye and made sure the focus was right before I pressed the shutter button and snapped several images. I followed Leo's finger and took pictures of everything he pointed out.

I zoomed in on the car's damage, trying to ignore the fur clinging to random parts of the grill and windshield.

Gross.

"Over here, Samantha," Leo said and pointed to the head. "Get a shot with the windshield in the image. This deer hit the grill then flipped up onto the hood and into the windshield."

I had to squat to do as he asked, and the entire time the beady eyes of the deer followed me. They were vacant and cold. Silly to get worked up about a deer, but this was my first time seeing death up close in real life.

I snapped shots of the damaged corner panel, likely the first spot of impact. My gut clenched, a sign something was off. Only I wasn't sure if it was with me or the accident.

The air was stuffy. Though a breeze was coming in off the river, none reached me. Remarkably, the tinny aroma of blood penetrated my snot-filled nose. Or I imagined it. Either was possible.

I gulped convulsively and looked away in hopes of resetting.

"Get a grip, Samantha," Leo mumbled.

I ignored the tightness in my stomach and focused on the job, desperate to be done so I could leave. I said, "I need to grab my ruler to put next to the um, er, on the hood for perspective?"

Leo patted the side pockets of his uniform pants. "We have a ruler somewhere."

A fresh layer of sweat broke out across my forehead, and drops ran down the back of my neck. I looked heavenward and tried to imagine puppies and happy kitties. Anything that wasn't gross or made my stomach roll. But I had nothing. All I could think about was the meat, the smell, and the deer's head.

"Got one," Leo said coming up behind me.

"Oh no." I couldn't turn and run because Leo was behind me to my right and the deer body was to my left. I lurched then cupped a hand over my mouth.

Vomit sprayed between my fingers and landed on the deer and car.

That explained my gut feeling.

"Crap," Leo said coldly.

CHAPTER TWO

"Judas H. Priest," Rawlings said. "You're worse than the rookie. Look what you've done."

I wiped my mouth with the sleeve of my sweatshirt. "Silver lining. At least the noodles from the soup I ate earlier can give us perspective. No need for a ruler." It was a bad joke, but all I had in response.

Humiliation didn't even cover how I felt. If the earth were to eat me alive right now, I wouldn't protest. I'd willingly jump into a sinkhole, an active volcano, or a giant shark's mouth. Stupid opportunity and its piss-poor timing.

Because I wasn't about to have this story be all about the barfing and not about the pictures, I continued to snap shots. After wiping my hand on my pants, of course.

Leo grabbed me by the arm. "C'mon. Get outta here before you mess everything up more than you already have."

He spun me away, and vertigo had me clutching his arm to keep from falling.

"You had no business coming out like this, Samantha." He hustled me toward LC.

"Then who would have taken your pictures?" Keeping his pace was hard. My feet dragged, and occasionally my big toe would snag on the pavement and I'd stumble. I continued to clutch Leo's arm for support as I bobbed and weaved toward my ride.

"I would have taken the pictures. We've done it before. Beats a drunk wanna-be photographer."

Stunned by his accusation, I stumbled, let go of his arm, and fell forward. My camera scraped the ground. I caught myself on my hands, thankfully, and didn't make a complete disgrace of myself by falling flat on my face. I refused to stay down. If I did, I'd give more fodder for Leo. I eased up to a stand since my balance was still wonky.

"I'm not drunk. I have the flu," I spat out my words with venom.

Leo snorted his disbelief. "Word is you and Precious have been hanging out at Junkie's now that she's of legal drinking age. You sure you didn't tie one on before coming here?"

Precious is my best friend. We've been tight since second grade.

"Shows what you know. Which, considering you're a cop, your observation skills suck. Looks like you aren't as skilled at everything as you think you are. Ha." I put extra emphasis on the last word, so much it made me cough. I pointed to my chest as I hacked into my hand.

When the cough subsided, I said, "See, I have a cough. Drunks don't have coughs."

He responded by opening LC's door and pointed for me to get in.

"If I'm drunk, should I be driving?" I said bitterly.

"Good point." He slammed the door.

"Oh, for Pete's sake." I tossed my hands in the air from frustration.

Leo brushed past me on his way to the patrol car. He took a bag from the trunk, then returned to me. Dropping the duffle bag at my feet, he riffled through it until he came out with a breathalyzer.

"For the love of all that's good and holy," I said. I sidestepped, but he blocked me.

"You say it's the flu? Prove it."

Oh, how I hoped he caught the virus and it

15

laid him out for days. I snatched the breathalyzer from his hand, then sucked in a deep breath before giving the small device a mighty puff.

Yeah, I was ticked at opportunity because I was standing here. I was ticked at myself for not tossing my cookies some place other than the accident scene. But I'd get over those. Growing up struggling to read had put me in several uncomfortable situations, and that school of hard knocks gave me a tough skin. However, what I would not get over was being treated like a degenerate by Leo Stillman.

"When you're done, give that to Junior," Rawlings said.

The breathalyzer beeped, and I showed the number to Leo.

"Ha," I said, then resumed my coughing fit. Deep breathing in and out was hard, my lungs heavy and full. Sucking in copious amounts of air had been a strain. One I was paying for now.

Leo took the device from me, read the numbers, then gave it a mad shake. "Must be broken."

I wanted to assault him with words, but was stuck coughing. As the coughing subsided, and I thought I'd get a word out, a new round would resume.

Leo smirked. "Looks like you have something to say but can't get it out. That's too bad."

As I hacked into my sweatshirt-covered elbow, I raised my other hand and stuck my middle finger in his face.

The small muscle in his jaw ticked twice. But before he could respond, the radio pinned to his shoulder chirped.

"Squad 50," said a male voice I recognized. Jeff Smith, one of three cops employed by Wind River and Leo's counterpart. Add the chief, a sergeant, and Lieutenant Rawlings, and that was the entire force.

A female voice responded, "Go ahead Squad 50."

"I'm at 5545 179th Avenue. Junkie's bar. I need medical attention for an unconscious, unresponsive, and breathing female, approximately forty-five years of age, with a possible upper body injury. I also need the fire department since she's pinned to a post by a car."

The female dispatcher said, "10-4 Squad 50, medical is on the way. Fire is on their way."

We all stood silent for a beat.

"Judas Priest," Rawlings said.

"Ms. Trina?" My eyes locked on Leo's face, searching for the answers to what wasn't said in the short conversation. It had to be Ms. Trina. She worked every Friday night at Junkie's bar. Friday's were theme night, and she'd once told me theme nights were her favorite. Smith had made it sound like her injury was serious.

"Holy crap," Junior said from behind me.

I turned and found him walking toward us, a towel pressed to his forehead.

"Did he say Ms. Trina was hurt?" Junior looked as shocked as I felt.

We'd all gone through school with Ms. Trina. As head lunch lady, she could tell when a student was having a bad day and gave us extra rolls, nuggets, or a Coke. Along with Leo's kid brother, Hue, I'd spent a fair amount of days getting extra's from Ms. Trina. Her oldest, Becca, was my age. Her youngest was in her final year of high school. Ms. Trina had become a single mom when her husband Bart had a massive heart attack back in February. Dropped dead in a convenience store near Century Link Field in Seattle following a Sounders Game. He'd reached for a bottle of water and died on the spot.

Ms. Trina was having a sucky year.

"You didn't go to Junkie's tonight?" I asked Junior. If I was a regular, so was Junior. He went as much as I did.

Junior winced. "I went for a while but left early because I had to be at work early today." His face tightened and he said angrily, "I bet this wouldn't have happened if I had stayed later."

He turned to Rawlings. "There were a couple of guys there that were getting rowdy. Didn't know them. They weren't from around here."

Rawlings said, "I'll want a statement about that later." He pointed a finger at me. "You sure you got pics of this, Samantha?"

I nodded, too numb to talk.

Rawlings directed his finger at Junior. "You call a tow truck?"

Junior nodded.

Rawlings said, "Then we're gonna leave now."

"Understood," Junior said. "My dad should be here soon anyway."

"I'll stay with you Junior until your dad comes," I said. It didn't feel right to leave someone out on the road alone in light of Ms. Trina's accident. How had a car pinned her to a post?

Rawlings grabbed me by my elbow and propelled me toward LC. "No can do, Camera-girl, you'll need to go with us. You're the on-call photographer. Try and keep up, too."

I glanced over my shoulder at Junior, Leo, and the scene. This was nothing compared to what I was about to see. I met Leo's stare and read his skepticism. He didn't think I was up for the challenge.

My mind flashed back to the pictures we'd

seen in class of crime scenes. Who had I been kidding about taking photos of a dead deer being a true test? No, my true test was about to come.

I climbed in LC and cranked his engine. I wrapped my arms around me as I waited for LC to warm up, a chill seeping deep into my bones.

LEO AND RAWLINGS sped to Junkie's bar. All I could think about was Ms. Trina and her family. The woman worked three jobs. Dad said her husband's life insurance must have sucked and followed the comment up with a lecture about the importance of retirement planning and insurance.

Junkie's bar was across town in the soon-to-be newer commercial development of Wind River. Crenshaw, Junkie's owner, knew this side of town was destined for expansion. He'd kicked off the impending boom by converting an old building on the corner of his junkyard into a bar. Currently, the property was surrounded by soon-to-be-demolished trees that fed into the foothills of Mt. St. Helens.

Crenshaw also happened to be the tow truck driver for the town. He was former military and vigilant about security. Some would even say paranoid.

Rawlings gestured out his window to the side of the road, and I took it to mean I should park there. I checked my camera's batteries and settings. Messing this up was not an option. I carried my crime scene kit with me.

An ambulance and a fire truck were parked ahead of us. Five people were standing at the head of Ms. Trina's car talking and gesturing. Two firemen, two EMTs and a cop.

"What's going on?" Leo barked.

One of the firemen looked our way. "She's pinned at the lower arm. Doesn't look good for the arm. Crenshaw is out of town, and the guy covering for him is about twenty minutes away on another pick-up. We're trying to decide how to move the car."

Smith, the cop who called it in, said, "Becca called dispatch and said her mom hadn't made it home. I rolled out here to see if she'd left. I found her chained to the pole, blindfolded, and with a gag in her mouth." He pointed to the back-corner panel of Ms. Trina's car. "From what I gather, it appears the place was robbed. Inside is a mess. They left Trina here, and in their haste to escape, they collided with her car, which pushed it into her."

I collapsed against LC. The fear and uncertainty of the situation left my knees weak. I'd never experienced violence and crime of this severity before. Up until now, my life was re-markably uneventful, and that's saying a lot when you're the daughter of a newspaperman and a lawyer.

"Her stats are falling," said the EMT moni-toring Ms. Trina.

Leo, Rawlings, and the other EMT had a brief discussion.

Leo turned to me. "Start photographing everything now. We're going to put her car in neutral and roll it back so we can move her." His words were hurried. The others were rushing to do what task they'd been assigned.

I brought the viewfinder to my eyes. The job of a forensic photographer was to take pictures of everything I could as they prepped to move Ms. Trina as well as shoot the move. This was done for court purposes. My photos would be evidence, and their value even higher if the un-thinkable happened and this became a homi-cide. I made sure to get shots of the scene as it was before they moved the car. Focusing the camera was hard with tears in my eyes. One thing for certain, we'd be at a different scene had the Crenshaw parking lot been different.

A few years ago, when Junkie's opened, the parking lot had been a gravel space and nothing more. Until an inebriated idiot who didn't know drive from reverse came inches from crashing into the building. After that, Crenshaw built nine small walls, one for each spot, each with a 4 ½ inch concrete pole called a bollard coming out of the center. Each was painted a bold color. Crenshaw's theory being, a wall took more idiocy to plow through and a speed bump wasn't a deterrent at all.

The walls, twenty inches high and two feet wide, were made from cinder blocks, and Ms. Trina was sitting on one. She hugged the red pole and, because of the shape of her VW Rabbit's front end, only her arm had been pinned from the hand to an inch below the elbow. Her leg escaped the same fate by centimeters. Had there been no wall, only a pole, the car would have crushed her.

Though Officer Smith had removed Ms. Trina's blindfold and gag, she remained unconscious. Seeing her chained to a pole broke my heart and sent tremors of fear through me. The awkward way her head hung back, her pallor, were reminiscent of corpse images I'd seen in school. This was not the vibrant, quick-to-laugh woman I'd known all my life. How had this happened?

A fireman named Bucky cut the chain. Smith bagged the chains as evidence.

On the count of three, the men worked in synchrony to move the car and Ms. Trina. I captured it all in stills. Within seconds, Ms. Trina was lifted onto the stretcher and the EMT's worked madly as they loaded her into the rig then sped away.

I stood next to LC while the cops discussed what to do next. A couple times Leo looked at me and nodded. At the patrol car, he took out a trash bag from the trunk.

I gulped, imagining all sorts of things he might put into the bag. Like Ms. Trina's white sneaker that lay a few feet from the pole.

Then he came to me.

Arms crossed, he said, "I'll take you from place to place and tell you what to get shots of. If at any time you think you might be sick, you throw up in this bag. You got it?" He thrust the bag at me.

"If you think I'm drunk and you have to use these pictures in a criminal case, wouldn't that be a possible problem for you?" My aim wasn't to get under his skin, but to fry whoever did this to Ms. Trina. Me being a technicality, the reason a criminal wouldn't be charged, was unacceptable.

"I have the breathalyzer that says you aren't. No one has to know I think it's broken."

I snatched the bag. "There's nothing left in my stomach anyway."

He grabbed me by the elbow. "Seriously,

Samantha. We can't have this scene messed up." His tone spoke to the seriousness of the situation. Not that I needed a warning.

I snatched my arm away. "Where do we start?"

Fevers were like tides. They burned hot when the tide was in and left a person clammy with uncontrollable shivers when it was out. Currently, the tide was out so I hit the shutter button several times on accident because of those shivers. The adrenaline didn't help. My flu symptoms were exacerbated by my nervousness. My hands shook, my breathing was shallow, and my stomach rolled with apprehension and upset.

"Breathe," Leo said. His focus remained on the area as he scanned for the next images to capture. He bagged evidence after I snapped the pics.

"I *am* breathing," I said and checked the display to make sure I had what I needed in the shot.

"No, you're panting. Breathe normally. Slow and steady."

He was right. I was a ball of nerves. There was no margin for error. The responsibility was a heavy weight to bear.

Rawlings said, "Come here, Samantha. I want shots from here. These pieces might be parts from the car that hit hers." Rawlings was standing next to Ms. Trina's car.

Smith came out from inside the bar. "Hey, I'm gonna need pictures in here, too. Looks like the robbers might have been the same people who've been hitting up the convenience stores and late-night diners."

The news called them the Comic Book Bandits and reported the robbers wore superhero masks when they held up a joint. It was also reported the Comic Book Bandits tied up the people and employees and left behind superhero novelty rings.

Leo gestured for me to follow Smith inside. The place had been tossed. Although, the theme tonight had been the seventies, one of the most popular themes for the bar, and the mess could have been from just that. The buffet with the pub food hadn't been cleaned, and plates had been knocked off, scattering food and broken ceramic everywhere. The disco ball hung above the center of the dance floor and continued to spin, shooting off a variety of colored lights. A blond afro wig balanced precariously at the edge of a bench seat of a booth.

"She didn't get any time to clean up." Captain obvious, that was me.

Smith surveyed the bar with disgust. "The kitchen's a wreck, too. Food pulled out of the fridge and everything." He pointed to the counter by the register. "Take a picture of that. Make sure to get the top." A red kid's party favor ring rested against the register. The sticker was a Batman emblem.

I spent the next two hours inside taking pictures. At one point, the Chief of Police joined our party.

When I stepped outside into the cool early morning air, the sun was peeking over Mt. St. Helen's, and exhaustion hit me hard. I was out of adrenaline, and the fever tide was in, raging, bringing with it waves of heat.

I stumbled to another parking pole and held onto it as I slid to the wall. I leaned against the cold metal and wondered how Ms. Trina was doing.

Shoes came into my field of vision, and I looked up to see my dad.

"What are you doing here?" My voice was hoarse. My throat dry.

"Covering this story. How you holding up, kiddo?" He pressed his hand to my forehead.

"You wouldn't happen to have any flu meds in your pocket, would you?"

"As a matter of fact, I do." He dug into his jacket pocket and handed me a tab with two capsules. From his other pocket, he took out a small bottle of water. "I heard you'd been called out to take pictures."

I swallowed the meds and chugged half the bottle.

Chief Louney joined us. "You know, Russ. You can't be asking Samantha to disclose anything that might affect this case." He turned his attention to me. "Do not speak to the press."

I gave him the thumbs up to show I understood his instruction. "I couldn't if I wanted to. It's all a blur. I'm tired and overwhelmed." Though Dad and I knew that wasn't true. All I had to do was think about one item in any photo I'd taken and my mind's eye could recall it as if looking at the actual space in real time.

Chief Louney said, "Then go home. You're done here."

Dad held out his hand and tugged me up. He pointed me toward LC and gave me a gentle shove.

I don't remember the drive home. Or climbing the stairs to my apartment over Dad's newspaper. I collapsed onto my bed, ready to get lost in a deep sleep.

But from the fever or not, restful sleep played elusive, coming only in short fits and bits with visions of evil superheroes.

CHAPTER THREE

Noon found me on the floor of my bathtub, the hot, steamy shower running over me. I was forced to exit when the water turned cold.

My lips were chapped to the point of cracking. My fever low enough for coherent thoughts.

I choked down a dose of flu medicine and transferred the photos from both scenes onto a thumb drive. Then I made myself as presentable as possible considering my fever was still one hundred and one. I pulled my hair into a ponytail and carried a hand towel in my sling bag to wipe off sweat for when the inevitable heat waves crashed over me again.

Dressed in navy blue leggings and a long yellow tunic, I added a dark gray hoody hoping it would hide the inevitable sweat stains. To stay in bed would be smart, but I was haunted by the images of last night. To make matters worse, my imagination was in full production, creating all sorts of creepy scenarios of what Ms. Trina had experienced while being robbed then chained to a pole.

Food of any variety was needed before heading out, though nothing in my sparse fridge looked appealing. Below my apartment was my dad's newspaper. Printing was done out of house, so by newspaper, I meant offices. More importantly, Dad kept a stocked fridge in the break room.

There were two stairways to my apartment. One at the front that led to the street. The other through a locked door at the outside rear of my apartment. That door opened to stairs that led directly into the back portion of the newspaper office.

The newspaper had one large room called the bullpen. Used to house cubicles for staff writers back in the day, now it was a large space with a conference table and chairs. Four separate rooms were off to the far-right side. One held files, archives, and supplies. The middle two rooms were my dad's office and the galley kitchen. The restroom was at the end.

Stella, Dad's office administrator who also worked the front, was at her desk by the lobby. An athletic woman with a penchant for herbal and natural remedies had, unfortunately, a past littered with dead husbands. Obviously, high blood pressure or other serious maladies couldn't always be controlled by an essential oil. Stella was on the phone, which allowed me to get to the kitchen unnoticed.

In the kitchen, the coffee pot was empty, an unusual occurrence for a newspaperman and company. The grounds were in the filter and water in the tank but no coffee. As if a cruel joke, someone forgot to flip the on switch. I punched the switch with a jab of my finger.

In the fridge was a tub of chicken noodle soup with my name on it. Literally. Someone had scrawled Sam in permanent marker on the container. I popped off the lid and stuck the entire container in the microwave, plastic and all.

While I waited, I sat at the small round table and flipped through the latest paper, Thursday's edition. Dad's paper, *The Wind River Journal*, came out in print Thursdays and Mondays. News could be read online daily for those who preferred.

When the microwave beeped, I took out the soup, putting it on the table.

The nutty aroma of the coffee filled the air and signaled it was done. I was pouring a cup, my other hand holding the mug, when Dad's sudden appearance startled me and I spilled scalding coffee all over my hand. I fumbled the carafe as I tried not to drop it on the counter in my haste to get to the sink.

"I knew I smelled you." His smile was smug.

I dashed to the sink and ran cold water over my hand. "Crap. What does that mean?" I gave my pits a whiff, but it was a lost cause considering how congested I was.

"I mean, I purposely left the coffee off so I'd know when you showed up."

That explained the smile.

He said, "Tough night, huh?"

I groaned. "The worst. I'm headed to the hospital to see Ms. Trina." The least I could do for a woman who'd constantly shown me kindness was to see if her family needed anything. And also, work hard to help the police put the people who did this to her behind bars. My fondness for justice, for wrongs to be righted, was entrenched in my character. Maybe it came from my mom being a lawyer and my dad a reporter. Or maybe because as a kid I was different and people wrongly stereotyped me. Regardless, I was going to see this through.

Dad poured himself a mug and topped off

mine, then reset the carafe back in its place. He set both mugs on the table and sat. "Poor Trina. She's had a run of bad luck. I hear she's in intensive care."

The sting from the burn had lessened. I turned off the faucet and searched through a kitchen drawer for salve. Stella was a freak about having natural medicines on hand. Sure enough, a tube made specifically for burns lay among the band-aids and oils.

"I couldn't sleep. I kept seeing all these images from the scene. I think I need to do something"—I waved my hand over my head—"to wipe my mind clean. Know what I mean?" Seeing scary stuff on TV was one thing. Seeing scary stuff in real life that affected people you knew and liked was entirely different. To say I was shaken was an understatement.

"You get used to it over time. Of course, some things never leave you, but that's how working in this business goes." His smile was sympathetic.

Did I want to be in this business?

Dad continued, "Lyle says Trina's deductible is incredibly high. A bunch of us are chipping in to help." Lyle Wagonknect was the town's auto and home insurance man. Bart Holland, Trina's husband, used to be the other one until he died.

From his shirt breast pocket, Dad took out a

piece of paper and offered it to me. "Are you feeling up to taking this to Bob's Body Shop? Tell him it's for Trina. Every bit counts for her."

It was a check for three hundred dollars.

"I hope they catch the guys who did this." I set the check on top of my sling bag, then sat across from Dad.

"Even if they find the guys, she won't recoup any expenses she'll incur because of this. These guys, these Comic Book Bandits, have worked their way down the state and have yet to be caught or get caught on tape. I doubt they're the sort to be insured or pay up if she sued them. And that's assuming they're the ones responsible for this."

"Poor Ms. Trina. I guess the silver lining in this is whoever these Comic Book Bandits are, they aren't violent." Last I read no one had been harmed in their robberies, only tied up, Trina's case being the worse. Had she been robbed by another group of criminals, the situation could have been much worse.

"Another silver lining? She wasn't working The Chief when it was hit three nights ago," Dad said. The Chief was a popular diner outside of town.

I dropped my spoon. "Graycloud's was robbed, too?" How had I not known this?

Walter Graycloud was one badass Native American who owned a scenic piece of land off the interstate and a big-wig with the Cowlitz tribe, who also happened to make the best homemade cinnamon rolls ever known to man. Not only did he own the diner, but a motel comprised of several small cabins that over-looked the Windy River. He even had a card room for the just-driving-through-gamblers in an ante-chamber off the diner.

"Yep," Dad said. "Apparently, Trina was sup-posed to work that night but switched with the other girl—I can't remember her name. Had she not switched days, she'd have been a victim twice."

Dad always had the inside gouge; it helped that he played poker with half the town. This made his reporting job easier.

I said, "The girl who works at The Chief is Jaime." She'd dated Hue, my other best friend in high school, I had talked to her a few days ago when I swung by and bought two cinnamon rolls. "Wait, you said three nights ago?"

Dad nodded.

Three nights ago was when I'd bought the rolls. I could've been at the diner when it was robbed, and if I hadn't gotten the flu, I would have been at Junkie's last night, too. A shiver of fear ran down my spine. This was too close for comfort.

"Why wasn't this in the news?" I asked.

Dad shrugged. "I kept it out of the paper by request of Graycloud and Chief Louney. Both wanted to keep it under the radar. Graycloud wanted to rule out the robbers were from the tribe."

"Oh, so it wasn't the comic book guys that robbed Graycloud's? I'd just assumed."

Dad held up his index finger and smirked. His way of announcing something good was about to be said. "Yes, the scene did look as if the Comic Book Bandits were the robbers, but Chief Louney believes the robbery was a copycat."

I pressed my palm to my temple in an attempt to process it all. "Are you saying whoever did this to Ms. Trina might have been a copycat and not these Comic Book Bandits on their crime spree?"

Dad nodded.

I was stunned. I'd assumed it was the Comic Book Bandits like the scene suggested. I'd have to remember this if I was going to use my PI license. What was that saying—assume makes an ass of you (u) and me? "Is keeping a lid on this smart? Shouldn't other businesses be warned?"

"The other businesses have been warned. Anything interesting in the pictures?"

This last question was Dad the reporter asking. I knew the difference because Dad the reporter was also Dad the poker player and king of his fantasy football league. Dad the poker player taught me everything he knew. And Dad the poker player had a tell. He flared his nostrils slightly when he had something up his sleeve. Just like he'd done now.

I shook my head. "I hope they're good enough in both cases. I'm dropping off a thumb drive before I head to the hospital." I blew on the soup as my stomach growled. Then said, "What are you looking for? Why are you asking about the pictures?"

Dad dismissed my question with a wave of his hand. He leaned closer and lowered his voice. "I heard from Chuck who heard from Lyle that Junior's car was stolen early this morning." Chuck owned the market next door and he, Lyle, and a few others played poker with my dad every week. They were worse than women when it came to gossip.

My mouth fell open. "What? How does that happen? Wasn't it towed to his dad's dealership? Junior manages the parts and service department, why didn't he put the car inside?"

Dad shrugged, indicating he was as puzzled

as me. "This isn't as uncommon as you might believe. I've covered stories of car theft rings. When you take the check down to Bob's ask him if he knows anything about this and let me know what he says."

I narrowed my gaze, suspicious. "Why am I asking? If this is a story, shouldn't you be asking?"

Dad's expression said nothing. He feigned innocence.

I wasn't buying it. "Come on, out with it."

"Bob lost money to me last week at poker, and he's still sore about it. If he gives you anything good, I'll follow up."

"If I do some digging for you, then I expect to get paid." We'd done this song and dance before. The truth was I had questions for Bob regardless of getting paid. But Dad didn't know that.

Dad eyed the tub of soup. "I'll take twenty-five bucks off your rent, and we'll throw the soup in as a perk."

"Deal," I said. I would have settled for the soup.

Dad held up a finger. "Ah, but I also want to see the pictures."

I grimaced. "Can I do that? Because I don't think I can."

"What if I happened to be looking over your

shoulder? Or maybe you leave your camera out and I help myself."

I rolled my eyes and tsked. "You've been in the reporting business a while, right, Dad?" I teased. "Because this feels amateurish."

Dad sighed heavily and sat back in his chair. "I'd love it if you'd confirm for me the robbery at Junkie's was a copycat, Sam."

"How could I do that? I'd have to know what makes one an original and the other a fake. Why not ask Crenshaw or Chief Louney?" I drank the broth from the container.

"Crenshaw doesn't know anything and Louney is buttoned up tight. There's more to this story."

"You're guessing. Speculating."

Dad raised a brow. "Am I? These robbers take Trina outside and chain her up to a pole. Which takes time. Then they peel out so fast they hit her car hard enough to push it into her?" He shook his head. "The pieces don't add up for me. All the other robberies, the people are tied up inside. Jaime was tied up inside the diner. Not outside."

"If this was the Comic Book Bandits, maybe they're mixing things up? Maybe they were spooked? Maybe they were in a hurry? Maybe they were afraid someone might come along?" I'd considered a thousand different scenarios in my need to understand this sense-less act.

Dad gave a skeptic shake of his head. "And if it was the copycat?"

"Then he tied her up outside because he's stupid and putting his own spin on it? He wants recognition for what he's done. After all, his robbery of Graycloud's diner wasn't in the paper. It was ignored." I'd learned this from true crime shows and maybe a bit from my class.

Dad nodded. "Yeah, that's why I think it's a copycat. Because these Comic Book Bandits are clever. They're calm and controlled. They've not been caught on store cameras. They've left no evidence other than what they wanted police to find. When you were inside Junkie's, did you see the plastic novelty rings they leave behind as their trademark?"

"Um." Chief Louney adamantly said to not talk to the press. Even though the novelty rings were a publicized fact.

Dad held up a hand. "Better yet, did you notice if a page from a comic book was left behind?"

Snapshots of the scene flashed in my mind's eye. "Nope." I clasped my hands over my mouth in horror as I realized I'd divulged information I wasn't supposed to.

Dad sat back in his chair and crossed his

arms, a smug smile on his face. "I shouldn't be telling you this, but Chief Louney slipped up and mentioned the comic book pages to me a few weeks ago. The cops have purposefully kept it out of the media. Graycloud's robbery didn't have the comic book page either."

My stomach dropped with dread. We were looking at a copycat. "Do you think that means whoever is doing this is from here? Someone we know?"

Dad's smile was large and toothy. "You bet it does. Oddities at the scene are clues, too."

I was appalled. "Why are you so happy about that?"

"I'm not happy these things are happening. I'm happy because this fool or fools aren't too bright and will likely get caught. I'll get point on the story. Makes for good press." Being a newsman, Dad covered stories that would haunt the average person, but he'd built up a thick shell. This was how I excused his enthusiasm. Like a thrill seeker craving a dangerous high, Dad needed stories more horrific than the last.

"Ugh, that's terrible. People were hurt."

"Samantha, honey, bad stuff happens. Happens all the time. Happens in the town you live in and is done by people you know. Shining a light on it is the only way to get the cockroaches to scurry back to where they came from."

We sat in silence, me slurping soup and Dad drinking coffee. Stuck on Dad's comments, my thoughts went to a darker place. Who among us would have done this, and did I really want to know?

CHAPTER FOUR

I left Dad's and drove to Junkie's. Crime scene tape roped off the parking lot and the door to the bar. I pulled LC in behind a patrol car parked on the side of the road.

I flung my sling bag over my shoulder after patting the front pocket to confirm the jump drive was there.

Seeing the scene in daylight would hopefully wash out the horrific images from the night before. Many of which had the creepy factor exaggerated by my imagination.

I didn't know how cops remained unbiased every day. I supposed only the good ones did.

Outside the bar, standing in the parking lot, were Crenshaw, the owner, and Leo. His uniform was crisp and clean, as if he hadn't been up a few hours before marking the crime scene.

Leo faced me, hands on hips. "What are you doing here?"

"I came out to see if any more pictures were needed." I took out the thumb drive and held it out to him. "Do you want these or do I need to take them to the station?"

"We're good for pictures." He took the small silver square. "I can take this in. Let me get you to sign something as proof of submitting." He moved away to his patrol car.

I focused on Crenshaw and was shocked by his appearance.

A big man, Crenshaw stood over six feet, was bald and solid with a belly that preceded him by several inches. A wall of stone. He usually wore threadbare flannel and typically sported a lumberjack's beard, only his beard was gone and his shirt, albeit still flannel, looked new.

"You look nice, Crenshaw." Dare I ask what the motivation for his new look was?

He shuffled awkwardly.

I did a quick subject change. "I'm sorry. What a mess to come home to. Have you heard anything?"

"Only that she's stable. She hasn't woken up yet." He pressed his lips together in a thin line.

"I can't believe this happened. Poor Ms. Trina."

Crenshaw said, "And she was out here by herself for who knows how long." His big shoulders shook as he held back tears. "If I didn't know this was done by those superheroes dumbasses, I'd put my money on Kevin Greevey."

He had my full attention. "That's interesting you would think Kevin did this. How come?"

Kevin's history of substance abuse was often the topic of gossip, usually instigated by some off-hand comment by Kevin's dad. If Kevin and Ms. Trina had a problem, I imagine the issue was either Ms. Trina cut him off or refused to serve him.

"I don't know. They were talking in hushed voices. Then Trina pointed to the door and told him to get out. I thought he might strike her. He was livid. I had to leave. I needed to be in Seattle. I showed Kevin the door, watched him drive away, and got on the road quickly after."

I took a stab at the timeline. "Wow, that's an early hour to get your drink on." My math had Kevin arriving at opening, five p.m.

Crenshaw nodded. He pointed to the front door of the bar. "He was standing outside when I opened the bar."

Leo approached and pointed a finger at me. "Stop talking to her. This is an open investigation and—"

I waved dismissively at Leo. "Oh, hush. What he's saying to me is nothing we wouldn't say if we met at Chuck's market in town. Can't you see he's distraught?"

Crenshaw bowed his head. "It's my fault. Becca called and said her mom hadn't made it home yet and wasn't answering her phone. I was...distracted. I didn't call the bar right away." He looked past my shoulder and cleared his throat. A pink tinge crept up his neck, his closely shaved neck. Clearly, the reason for his appearance change was a woman.

"If I were on a date with someone I liked, I would've been distracted as well. And who would have ever expected this"—I swept my hands toward the crime scene tape—"to have happened?"

"Do you even date? "Leo mumbled.

"I date guys who aren't buttheads," I said. "As you can imagine, those are hard to find. Like the elusive Bigfoot."

Crenshaw continued, "Even when I called the police and asked them to do a drive-by, I underplayed my concern. I'll never be able to forgive myself if something happens to her."

I patted his arm. I was contagious after all. "You did everything you could do. Stop beating yourself up."

He nodded and cleared his throat. "Speaking of Bigfoot, you want to see the video, Leo? It's grainy, but I can't come up with any other reasonable explanation than Bigfoot."

"Bigfoot?" I had to know.

Crenshaw nodded. "One of my cameras caught a hairy leg coming out of the bar shortly after closing time."

My heart beat madly with excitement. "Seriously, that's cool. You can't tell anyone, though, because then you'll have everyone out here camping and trying to catch sight of Bigfoot." The Pacific North West hosted no less than four different Sasquatch research groups. One was housed near St. Helens, which was the backdrop for Junkie's.

"Which is exactly why I asked you not to say anything, Crenshaw. Her dad owns the local paper." Leo sighed in defeat.

I made like I was zipping my lips. "I totally won't tell my dad. Unless of course word starts to get out, and he'll hear it anyway."

Leo groaned. "You done here, Samantha?" Leo asked. "Because I'm not."

I took the hint. He didn't want to talk to Crenshaw with me present.

"I'm headed to the hospital. I'll let you know if there's been any change," I said to Crenshaw.

I paced my walk to LC, scanning the area for anything I might have missed in the dark.

Leo caught up to me. "I hope you give this experience serious consideration. I'm not sure you've got it in you to take photos of scenes. Rawlings and I submitted your performance evaluation to your professor today."

I stopped by LC's hood and put my hand on the top, leaning against it because I was slightly winded. The flu was moving into a chest cold.

I fanned at the beads of sweat on my forehead. "Let me guess. You were less than flattering with your evaluation of my skillset. Even though I did two scenes, and neither was something as simple as taking pictures of a wrecked car. And also, you evaluated me before seeing the pictures." Dick move in my opinion.

"I said you're skilled. But I also said I don't think you're cut out for this. You're too personally involved."

"This scene is personal. I grew up with Ms. Trina." Who was he to tell me how to feel?

Leo crossed his arms and stared down his nose at me. "Every scene is personal. What if Junior had been killed by that deer?"

Something I hadn't considered.

"Or maybe you get called out to take a picture of a scene of someone you don't know. But that scene is personal to the people who are impacted by it. Maybe they've lost a loved one. You can't unsee what happens out here, Samantha. It'll leave you jaded. It'll change you."

I was worried about that exact same thing. But this was my life. He didn't have a say in it. I studied him. "You seem to be doing okay. Or is it your natural buttheadedness helps you deal with being jaded?"

Had I not taken flu medicine with the possible side effects of hallucinations, I could have sworn Leo's lips twitched in what was the hint of a smile.

He briefly ducked his head then looked at me. "My people have struggled for decades. My brothers and I have spent years working with our mom on the reservation. I've been up close and personal with addiction and mental illness. I learned early on, a rosy tint on life was an illusion. I know you think my life has been all about football, touchdowns, cheerleaders, and itchy jocks. But this is gritty business, and I've been aware of it since I was a kid."

He was right. I did think his life was rosy. Everything came easy to him. And though I was close to his younger brother, I had no idea what happened on the reservation. Not wanting him to see he'd rattled me, I went for levity. "Had you washed your jock more often, maybe it would've itched less. Which is gross, by the way."

His expression of confusion would have made me laugh had the reason for us interacting not been serious. He couldn't figure me out, and I was okay with that. Here he'd told me something personal and serious, and I'd gone for the easy joke. Taking pictures of a crime scene wasn't a laughing matter. And yeah, I questioned if I was up for it. But the only way to know was to see this through.

I knocked on LC's hood twice to signal a change in subject. "Speaking of crime scenes—"

"You are not to speak to anyone about these crime scenes. Not even Precious. I know that'll be hard for you, but give it a try." His expression was stern.

I gasped. Precious was my best friend. I told her everything. "How dare you insinuate I can't keep a secret?"

He rolled his eyes. "You were saying about crime scenes?"

Crap. How was I supposed to tell him about Graycloud's being robbed without proving I sucked at secret keeping?

I pressed my lips together as I contemplated my move. Unable to breathe through my nose because of my congestion, I blew out the breath in frustration. "I have something to tell you. You, Leo, not you, the cop."

"Why me Leo? What's the difference?"

I huffed then mumbled, "Because what I have to tell you is not common knowledge."

"Is it a secret?"

Slapping that smug smile off his face would have felt awesome. But striking an officer in uniform was begging to be arrested for assault.

"I'm only divulging what I know because I think it has something to do with this." I jerked my thumb behind me toward the bar.

Leo became serious. "I'm listening."

"When you're off duty, put on regular clothes and go to Graycloud's. Ask him about what happened a couple nights ago."

He looked skeptical. "That's what you're giving me?"

"I'm assuming you can put two and two to-gether and figure out what I'm saying." I did the wide-eyed-don't-be-stupid look.

He jerked his head toward Junkie's. "Gray-cloud would have reported something like this."

"Would he?" I said with sarcasm. "Because he didn't." I knocked on LC's hood again. "I'm out. If you need me to take more pictures, let me know." I shuffled to the driver's side.

"You should be home in bed," he said.

I gasped in mock surprise. "What? Are you

saying you think I wasn't hungover?" I climbed in and slammed the door.

He crossed his arms. "In bed works for hangovers, too." He nodded toward LC. "He needs oil."

I turned the engine over, and LC sputtered to life. "What else is new?"

CHAPTER FIVE

I drove into Vancouver (Not British Columbia, but Washington) to the hospital where they'd taken Ms. Trina. Helping the family any way I could was a high priority.

There I met Precious. Her real name is Erika. We'd bonded during second grade when we, Hue included, realized that we were the only kids pulled out of class for extra support. Precious went to speech therapy for a wicked stutter that only showed up now when she was tired and overly stressed. Her nickname came when a bully from our class asked her what was so special about her that she didn't have to read in front of the class, and she'd responded with, "Because I'm P-p-precious." The moniker stuck. Yeah, at first it was used to tease her, but the truth was eventually seen. She embodied the nickname. The girl treated everyone like they had a gift to give to the world and, in return, she was treated the same.

Precious was standing outside the double sliding doors of the hospital. Dressed in a black skirt with a simple white shirt and black flats with her pale blond hair pulled back into a bun. Typically one for bolder colors, she looked like she'd come to hand out Bibles, or for reasons more depressing. Like maybe she was the Angel of Death. Precious stood slightly over six feet with sparking blue eyes and alabaster skin.

"You look like poop," she said when she spotted me shuffling toward her.

"I feel better than yesterday. Why are you wearing your funeral skirt?"

Precious liked to have certain outfits for specific events. She said dressing correctly for the occasion gave people confidence and inner strength. I'm guessing she was feeling as shaken up by these turn of events as I was.

She said in a hushed voice, "You said it was bad."

I lowered mine to match. "She's not dead. Or in danger of dying." At least not that I knew of. "Guess what I heard?"

Precious raised her brows in anticipation.

Keeping my voice low, I said, "Crenshaw said his video caught a hairy leg coming into the bar right before it closed." Bigfoot was Precious's secret interest. He'd been her imaginary friend back in elementary school. Imagine her glee to grow up and discover he might actually exist.

Her eyes widened. "Do you think...could it be?"

I shook my head. "I mean, why would Bigfoot rob the bar and chain up Ms. Trina? What's he gonna do with the money?" I pretended to give her question thought. "Though, food was everywhere like someone had gone on a feeding frenzy."

"Someone being a giant hairy man-like beast?"

I laughed. "Or bear or crazy vandals high on something."

She frowned at me. "You're a buzz kill."

"I like to keep things real." I winked.

She clasped her hands together, signaling she'd come to a decision. This was her tell, and I knew from experience only a miracle would sway her from further pursuing this angle. "We have to find out if it was a Bigfoot. Letting this drop because you think it's unlikely isn't good enough for me."

"I'll leave you to figure out how we'll go about it then." I gestured for us to go into the hospital.

Precious looked past me and nodded her

chin in that direction. "Didn't you say Junior was in an accident, too?"

I nodded. "Hit a deer."

"I wonder if he was admitted. Because Kevin Greevey is lurking by the ER doors."

I turned to my left. The hospital was L-shaped. The doors to the main wing were dead center of the long line in the L. The ER was at the end of the short part. Kevin Greevey was standing by an ambulance, watching the doors of the ER. His hands were stuffed into his pockets, his right leg bouncing to a frenzied beat only he could hear.

"Why is he just standing there?" Precious asked. "Maybe gonna try and steal some drugs?"

I rolled my eyes. Kevin didn't strike me as being that stupid, but then addiction made smart people do stupid things. "Maybe he's waiting for someone?" A guess on my part.

"Should we go in?" Precious pointed to the door.

We both moved toward the door but stopped before entering.

I glanced over my shoulder again. "He looks jumpy."

"Dope will do that to a person," Precious said.

Kevin shifted his weight and glanced at his watch. Definitely waiting for someone or something to happen. Call it curiosity or straight-up nosy, I wanted to know who or what.

My answer came a second later when Becca Holland came out of the ER doors. She scanned the drop-off area, then moved toward Kevin when she spotted him. He sprung forward and rushed to her, wrapping her in his arms. Becca collapsed against him, hugging him tightly around the waist.

"Whoa," Precious said. "When did they start dating?"

"Um, last I heard she kept too busy to date." Ms. Trina had recently told me this one night at the bar. "Focusing on college and all that."

I pushed Precious toward the door. "Let's go inside and see how Ms. Trina is doing. We'll figure out what's going on between them next." On the elevator ride up, I filled in Precious on what Crenshaw had said.

Ms. Trina was in the intensive care unit. The nurse guarding the door was adamant about us not getting one step closer, family only.

"Only her family is outside hugging the man who might have put her here," Precious mumbled as we took seats on a bench along the wall. We decided to wait for Becca to return. Fifteen minutes later, she did.

Becca was a mini version of her mother, minus the frosted hair. Becca kept hers their natural chestnut, whereas Ms. Trina added frosted blond highlights. Both women wore their hair to the mid back. Both women were farm-girl pretty. Ms. Trina had aged well and Becca would, too. I, on the other hand, looked like my father and was constantly worrying about the rate his hairline was receding.

Becca came out of the elevator, saw us, and stopped short. "Hey."

I leapt to my feet. "Becca, we're so sorry. We wanted to know if there's anything we could do to help?"

Tears glistened in her red-rimmed eyes, and she wiped at them with her index finger. "No. We're in a holding pattern. The doctors have her stable, but they had to remove her hand and part of her arm. She hasn't woken up."

Whoa.

Precious guided her to the bench, then sat beside her, rubbing her back. I kept my distance as I didn't want to pass along my germs.

"Have you heard from the police?" I asked. "Leo was at Junkie's this morning."

"Nothing new. I'm thankful I called Crenshaw when Mom didn't show up. How long would she have sat out there had I not noticed she hadn't come home?" Her voice caught on a sob. She buried her face in her hands.

I lived alone. My place might be over my

dad's business, but that didn't mean we constantly saw each other. How many days would go by before my parents noticed I wasn't home? "Is that something you did, made sure each other showed up when you were supposed to?"

Becca sucked in a deep breath and nodded. "Mom says we can't be too careful. Other than children, women are always targets. We did what we could to protect each other."

I glanced at Precious because, like me, she lived alone with no one checking on her daily. "Smart. Maybe Precious and I will do something similar."

Precious nodded her agreement. Neither of us wanted to be victims.

I continued, "I'm sorry about her arm and hand."

Becca nodded. "The doctor said she's lucky. Had the car hit her body, she might not have survived."

"Can I get you something to eat, Becca? Coffee?" Standing there idly added to my helpless feelings.

"I don't know if I can eat," Becca said.

"When was the last time you tried?" Precious was persistent.

I said, "I'll get you some snacks and water. Nothing heavy. You have to take care of yourself. I'm guessing you're taking care of your sister?" Becca had a younger sister still in high school.

She nodded. "People have brought food to the house, and my mom's friend is hanging out there. She'll relieve me here in a few hours."

I trudged off to the cafeteria and bought trail mix, a banana, and a large bottle of water.

Kevin Greevey was sitting at a table in the corner, drinking coffee. Unable to control my insatiable curiosity, I slid into the chair opposite him and said, "I'm grabbing Becca snacks. Does she like trail mix or is she not a mixed nut person?"

Kevin looked at the package and said, "She hates dried fruit. You're better off getting her graham crackers."

Of all the Greevey men, Kevin was the best looking. He had piercing blue eyes, chiseled features, and looked like a Hollywood A-list leading man. But his reputation was dark and his mannerisms brooding. And there was the whole drug addiction thing.

He slapped his hand angrily against the table. "Dammit, Samantha. How did you know I was here for Becca?"

"I saw you two outside by the ER. Initially, I assumed you were here for your brother until she came outside."

He looked puzzled. "Why would my brother be here?"

Now it was my turn to be surprised. "You know he hit a deer last night, right? Deer came through the windshield and knocked him out. When I saw you, I thought he might have had complications. Had to come here and was under observation."

Kevin rolled his eyes. "Please, if Junior the Great needed anything, Daddy would make sure he'd have it from the comfort of home."

"Junior still lives at home?" I knew he lived in the same general area as where he grew up, but I'd assumed he'd bought a house by his dad. In high school, he'd been voted "In command of his destiny and going places." Not the typical basement dwelling college grad who mooched off his parents.

"Why would he give up the cash cow?" Kevin took my bag of trail mix and tore it open, then wolfed down half by pouring it into his mouth.

"You did," I said.

Or maybe he hadn't had a choice, given his history. Rumor was he'd boost a car or ten for parts and fast cash. Rumor also said this was how he funded his drug habit. Not the kinda guy Becca Holland typically dated.

"Because I can't abide by rules. Or at least rules I think are dumb." He finished off the trail mix. His body was stiff, his gaze narrow. He was strung tight, ready to spring. Bruises were on the knuckles of his right hand, a sign he'd been in a fight. Crenshaw hadn't said he'd hit Ms. Trina but Crenshaw hadn't been there when she'd closed up.

I went for broke. I figured if he hurt me, we were in a hospital, so I'd get quick service. "Heard you and Ms. Trina had it out yesterday at Junkie's."

Kevin glared at me. "Oh, yeah? Where'd you hear that?"

I shrugged, not committing. "Around. What was it about?"

He leaned forward and snarled, "None of your goddamn business."

"I'm not the only one who'll ask you about this. You know that, right?"

When he sucked air in through his nose, his nostrils flared. "What I know is you won't hear the truth in what I have to say. Your mind's made up about me and last night. Now, I have to convince you otherwise. Guilty until proven innocent. And you know what I have to say to that? Hm?"

I shook my head.

"I say you can go fu—"

I jumped to my feet, forcing the table back toward him. "Alright, I get the point. Consider this a friendly heads up." I scurried away from the table, uneasy.

When I glanced over my shoulder, Kevin's angry stare was focused on me. Anger was likely his default emotion. And he was right—I did want him to convince me he hadn't played a part in the robbery and assault on Ms. Trina.

CHAPTER SIX

Bob's Auto Body was two blocks east of Wind River city center. Closest parking spot for LC was a block away. By the time Precious and I hoofed it from our cars to the shop, I was winded. The flu meds were wearing off, and a nap sounded heavenly.

Bob's real name is Adam, but twenty years ago he bought Bob's from the original Bob and never changed the name. As a joke, people called him Bob and it stuck.

The shop was a three-bay garage with an office attached. Two of the bays were open, and Bob was standing in front of the bays drinking a coke.

He gave us a head nod as a greeting.

"My dad asked me to bring a check to help cover expenses for Ms. Trina." From my purse, I took out the check and two twenties. "I have this to contribute, too."

"Here's my contribution." Precious handed him a wad of cash, many of the bills ones. She worked nights in her parent's restaurant and it was probably her tip money.

He dropped his can, squashed it with his foot, then picked it back up. "Come on, I'll get you ladies a receipt."

I glanced into the bays. Ms. Trina's car was in the third bay with the door closed. "Do you think it'll take a lot to fix her car?" I followed him into an office that held two customer chairs, grease stains complimentary, an old wood desk, a dirty chair behind the desk, a computer, and a Seahawks calendar.

Bob plopped in a chair behind his desk and stretched. "Nah, shouldn't be too bad. The kids I have from the school are talented mechanics and auto body guys."

Bob offered on-the-job experience for kids aspiring to work in his industry.

A memory from the past sprung forward. "Hey, wasn't Kevin Greevey in that program?"

For me, the rumors about Kevin weren't aligning with the Kevin I'd talk to today. At the hospital, I'd seen an angry guy, not a twitchy drug guy. Though my experience with druggies was limited to portrayals on TV.

Bob nodded and took a notepad out of a

drawer. "Kevin's a natural with a car. If he went into business with his dad and brother, they'd have an empire." He gave a sad shake of the head. "Too bad what they say about him."

"That he's a druggy?" Precious asked.

Bob's head snapped up, and he looked between us both. "Most asinine rumor I've heard yet." He shook his head in frustration. "Just can't see Kevin being a druggie. Too tightly wound to give up control. But he's one heck of mechanic." He finished writing the receipts then ripped them from the pad. He handed one to each of us.

"Do you see him coming unwound enough to tie someone to a pole and leave?" Dad was right, tying her to the pole didn't make sense.

Bob shook his head, skepticism on his face. "No, I can't see him doing that. I can see him getting mad. Even shouting at someone and throwing a punch. But to tie someone up? Nah, that comes from a deep-down craziness, and Kevin doesn't have that. What he has in spades is anger toward his family."

"Because his brother is perfect," Precious said. "My sister is perfect, too, and sometimes it's super annoying. Same for Rachel, right, Sam?"

Rachel was my older sister. A recent college graduate in nursing, she'd signed over four years of her life to the US Navy. "According to my mom, 'Rachel isn't perfect. She's ideal.' "

"Same thing," Bob said.

"I know, but I pretend it's not, or else I'd be constantly frustrated with Rachel." I was not the ideal daughter. Not because I was naughty, but because much of my school career had been a struggle, whereas Rachel had breezed right through everything. "But I don't hate Rachel. Even if I am frustrated with her."

Bob said, "Because your parents don't play you two against each other like Senior did and still tries to do. Always trying to get one son to up the other. Seen it here myself. Came here to get Kevin riled about being out-performed by Junior. Senior hated that Kevin was working for me and didn't take the work-study program from his dad's dealership or brother's repair shop."

"Is that why he got kicked out of his house?" Precious was more in the know than I was.

Bob guffawed. "As if. Senior loved telling everyone he kicked Kevin out, but the truth is Kevin left on his own. Happened shortly after graduation."

I added pieces of Kevin's past together. "Then Kevin worked here a while, didn't he? Beyond the school program?"

Bob nodded. "And I'd still have him here had

he not up and quit. Said he had a better gig. He was a whiz with classic and exotic car restoration."

"He's rumored to be boosting those types of cars," I added.

Bob frowned. "Restoring them, yeah. Stealing them for parts? Can't see it. Kevin is a craftsman. An old soul." His brow furrowed and he squinted. "I just can't see it."

This was not the picture of Kevin everyone else painted. Perhaps Kevin's anger came from stealing the classic cars he loved but not restoring them.

I steered us in a different direction. "Do you mind if I look at Ms. Trina's car? I took the pictures at the scene, and I'd like a second look to make sure I got everything." I wasn't planning on taking more pictures. If I did, they'd likely be inadmissible since the car had been moved. Even though Bob's was technically the police compound for our small town. A look again might be worth it.

Bob gestured for us to help ourselves.

Rising from the chair, I said, "Hey, did you hear Junior's car was stolen last night? First, he hits a deer only to have his car stolen after he tows it to his place of employment. Talk about having a bad night."

Bob rose, too, and walked behind us as we

exited his office. "I'm not surprised it was stolen. Happens a lot with that specific tow truck driver."

I glanced at him over my shoulder. "What do you mean?"

Bob snorted in disdain. "Maybe I should say it's a combo of the tow truck company delivering to Greevey's dealership. This is not the first car this guy has towed that's been stolen off the dealership lot. People think Crenshaw is crazy with all his cameras and fencing, but cars he tows and stores don't get stolen."

Precious said, "Maybe it's because they're stored at a junkyard and people assume everything there is junk."

Another snort from Bob. We must be making his day with our lack of knowledge. "Junkyards are like a giant treasure chest filled with gold. People get rid of stuff without checking its value. Crenshaw once had a guy donate an old 1969 Mach 1 Mustang. Yeah, it was in bad condition, but once restored, Crenshaw sold it for over fifty grand. People are stupid."

"What?" Precious and I said in unison.

Bob looked pleased with our surprise and rapt attention. "Yeah, people inherit stuff and have no idea what it is. That old mustang was in a barn out by the Columbia Gorge buried under hay, old tarps, and bird crap. The guy who in-herited was trying to sell the land and needed the barn torn down. All he could see was the big sale of the land and not the gem of a car."

"Wow," I said. "No wonder Crenshaw's junk-yard is under tight security. Who knew?"

"Me." Bob pointed at his chest. "I knew."

I didn't bother telling him my question was rhetorical. "When will you start working on Trina's car?"

Bob said, "In a few days I'll probably get the okay to start. Typically, the police will want to take another look even though they'll take the panel when it comes off." He mumbled the last part.

"Oh, I thought maybe insurance was holding it up," I said.

We stopped short of the bay that held Ms. Trina's car. A large thick plastic sheet separated her car from the others. A sign-in log on a clip-board hung from a nail in the wall. Bob handed it to me to sign.

He said, "Her deductible is incredibly high, sadly. More of this will come out of pocket than from the insurance."

Precious said, "That's funny considering her husband was an insurance man. Maybe he knew something we don't."

Bob shrugged. "Bart didn't keep his deductible this high. I think it's something Trina changed after he died. Bart wasn't a gambler and said high deductibles were like flirting with danger, asking for an accident to happen."

"Why would she change it?" I asked.

Bob said. "Usually people do it to save money."

Now I understood. Saving money was never a bad idea. Maybe I should change my deductible. "Does a high deductible affect how quickly your car gets fixed?"

Bob said, "No, repairs slow down when more than one insurance company is involved or getting approval for OEMs. Sometimes parts are out of stock, too."

"OEMs?" Precious asked.

"Original Equipment Manufacturer, basically brand-named parts," Bob explained.

I needed clarification. "As opposed to generic parts?" I guessed generic parts made sense. Nearly everything had a generic version these days.

"Yep," Bob said. "OEMs are pricier and require insurance approval."

I signed the log-in then ducked under the plastic. At Ms. Trina's car, I stared at the corner panel that had crushed her arm. Everything about this situation was unsettling.

Precious pointed to reddish pink stains on Ms. Trina's car. "Is that blood?"

Ms. Trina's car was red. Not a hot-rod red but the typical compact car red. Boring red.

Bob slipped on a pair of readers and leaned in close. "Nope, paint. Maybe transferred from the pole."

I pointed to a smudge of brown. "That's blood."

Precious looked at the car, then me. She paled. Several tiny brown smudges were scatted across a large portion of the panel.

I looked at the indentation in the car. It was slight. How fortunate that only the corner caught her. It was enough to crush her arm, but it could have been worst. "She's lucky. All things considered."

"Ain't that the truth," Bob said. "Had she been sitting anywhere else, had the car been clipped anywhere else, she might not have lived. It's not every day a two-thousand-pound vehicle gets pushed into someone and only does damage to a small part of the body."

I pictured last night, adding the image of the car fleeing the scene and hitting Ms. Trina's. "Do you think the car that clipped hers peeled out at high speeds?"

He shrugged. "Depends on the offending car and how close her car was parked."

I mentally scrolled through the pictures I'd taken. Ms. Trina drove a VW Rabbit. "Based on the skid marks, her car had been parked inches from the pole."

"Wouldn't take a lot then," Bob said. "Based on the damage, my guess is the car that hit her was bigger, slightly heavier, so not as much speed was needed as you might think."

I moved to the other end where her car had been hit. Two colors. Both red. They'd been hard to see in the morning hours, even with the lights. Too many shadows.

I pulled my phone out of my bag. "Do you mind if I get a few more pictures. I want to compare them to what I took last night."

Bob gestured for me to go ahead.

The phone's camera quality was lacking, but it would have to do. I wasn't my father's daughter for nothing. Bob's remark about rub-off paint made me want to see if any color had rubbed off from the hitting car. Just in case my pictures were bad, I wanted a few backups.

CHAPTER SEVEN

The next morning came, and with it, a fever-free body. My fever broke somewhere in the middle of the night. Being on the other side of an illness is glorious even if it leaves you a sweaty, greasy mess. A problem fixed with a shower.

Eating toast with peanut butter, I loaded the photos from my phone to my computer and compared them to what I took the night of the robbery. My gut about the shadows had been spot on. Though the stains and paint rubs could be seen in my original images, the new ones gave them the definition the originals lacked. I printed out both sets, wrote up an explanation for the images, including how and when they were shot, tucked them in a manila envelope, and stuck them in my sling bag to drop off at the police station.

I dressed in jeans, Ugg's, a long fluffy sweater in army green, and pulled my hair back into a ponytail. Two minutes with my makeup bag put color on my previously sallow complexion.

Out the window were gray skies and drizzling rain. Soon, those rare sunny autumn days in the PNW would be pushed aside for endless misty rain. Wearing a light gray North Face raincoat, I walked the pictures over to the police station two blocks from my apartment.

Inside, Pamela Hopkins, police clerk, manned the front desk. The waiting room chairs were empty.

"Hey," I said. "How's it going?" She'd graduated with my sister, Rachel, and they'd been on the volleyball team together.

"It's going." She gave a sad shake of her head.

"Everything okay?" I fumbled with my sling bag and took out the pictures.

She sighed wearily. "What's this world coming to? Ya know, if I didn't work here, I wouldn't believe half of what I've seen."

Yeah, Leo had a point about always looking at the underbelly of life. Consistent exposure changes a person, sometimes not for the best. I held up the manila envelope. "I have pictures for Leo or Rawlings. Either around?"

She jerked her head to the door behind her

that separated the lobby from everything else. "Leo is. He's in the back. Rawlings is off today, but I'm sure they'll call him in now that we're shorthanded." She pressed a button, and a loud buzzing sound filled the space, indicating the door lock had released. I hustled to get to it before she let go.

Pulling the door open, I said, "Thanks. I hope your day gets better."

"Doubtful," she said over her shoulder.

Behind the door was quiet. The Wind River Police force was comprised of seven people. I didn't expect the place to be hopping like portrayed on a TV show. Those were typically big city stations. The office portion of the station was an open room with six cubbies making a square in the center of the room. To the left was a hallway lined by a row of offices. The first office belonged to Chief Louney. The second office was for interrogations. A one-way mirror was cut into the center of the wall looking into the room.

I circled the cubbies but found no Leo. I found his desk. No surprise his was organized, spotless, and devoid of personal items. Burned coffee was the main scent of the station. The other unidentifiable scents that followed weren't as pleasant. Since there wasn't any coffeemaker out by the cubbies, I figured a break room had to be down the hall.

As I passed the interrogation room, I glanced through the mirror. Expecting the room to be empty, I was shocked to see Chief Louney standing and pointing, yelling at Officer Smith. Smith was in uniform slumped in a chair, his head hung low, his shoulders hunched. The room was soundproof. Next to the mirror was a small intercom box with an on/off button and a dial for volume.

I checked to see if I was alone as I contemplated pressing the ON button. How would I explain the eavesdropping? At a police station, for cripes sake. Smith was getting his rear end chewed out. Did it have to do with Ms. Trina's case? He'd been the first officer on the scene. I glanced at the intercom. My finger itched to press the ON button. I was reaching out for it when Leo came out of another room at the end of the hallway.

"Samantha?"

I jerked my hand back. "I didn't touch it."

"Good. Because it's none of your business." He came toward me, a mug in his hand.

I jerked a thumb to the window. "Is he getting his performance evaluation? Because I don't think it's going well."

Leo's expression remained nondescript. "What brings you here?"

I held up the envelope. "I took money to Bob's to help Ms. Trina and looked at the car again. I was worried about shadows on the original pictures so I took a few more. In here are both sets. The new ones were taken with my cell phone. The quality is meh, but shows the damage more clearly. I think the car that hit hers was red."

The door to the interrogation room opened, and Chief Louney stepped out. His face was red, and sweat dotted his forehead. He slammed the interrogation room door with such force the mirror shook. He pointed to Leo. "Let him sit in there and stew. You understand me?"

"Yes, sir."

"No food, no water. Nothing. When he gets control of himself, let me know."

Leo and I looked into the room. Smith was blubbering into his hands.

Louney turned to me. "And I better not see your dad here probing me about why we're questioning one of our own in the robbery case. I'll call him when I'm ready. Do you understand me?"

"Yes, sir." I held up the envelope. "I was only dropping off more pictures of Ms. Trina's car. The new images show two different color red paints. From what Bob told me, I'm guessing one is a rub off."

Louney pointed to Leo. "Smith's off duty vehicle is red, isn't it? Find it and see if it has damage. See if you can find a link between him and Kevin Greevey."

I couldn't believe my ears. Jeffrey Smith did this to Ms. Trina? The guy who cried half of kindergarten year because he couldn't be separated from his mom? My mind stumbled over the probability, generating a thousand questions.

Louney stomped into his office and slammed the door behind him.

I faced Leo, incredulous. "I don't believe it."

Leo cleared his throat and crossed his arms. "It's not up to you. The facts will speak for themselves."

I scowled. "You believe a guy you worked with posed as one of the Comic Book Bandits and robbed Junkie's, then chained Ms. Trina to a pole and sped away."

"Sped away because he was flustered. As the nearest on-duty officer, he'd been called to the Greevey accident."

"But you were at the Greevey scene." I stated the obvious because I was digesting what he'd divulged.

"That's because Smith couldn't be raised on

the radio. Earlier he'd gone on a call out past Junkie's for some kids drag racing. Rawlings and I were farther out by Graycloud's, but because dispatch couldn't get Smith to acknowledge, Rawlings and I had to respond."

"Oh," I said in defeat. "And I suppose, one could speculate, that there were no kids drag racing and the person who called in the complaint about the kids was Smith's accomplice."

I fitted the pieces together. Smith's accomplice, possibly Kevin Greevey, called in a bogus complaint, and Smith went out. This gave Smith a reason for being in the area and time for him and his accomplice to rob Junkie's. When the call came in for Junior's accident, Smith and his accomplice were busy cleaning out Junkie's and tying up Ms. Trina. Smith didn't answer. Leo and Rawlings were sent out to Junior's accident instead. Smith, being a police officer, had known that the Comic Book Bandit robberies were done by more than one person. He'd also known what was left behind at the scene.

"Wait." I shook my head, trying to shake a nagging thought loose. "My dad said the Comic Book Bandits leave a page from a comic book behind at every scene. There were no comic book pages at Junkie's." None that I saw. Dad said none at Graycloud's either. Wouldn't Smith know that? If he was trying to blame the Comic

Book Bandits, wouldn't he make sure to leave pages at the scene?"

Leo looked down as if my question required serious consideration. After what felt like the longest minutes in eternity, he sighed heavily and looked at me. "I don't have an explanation for that. It's a loose thread." He then pressed his lips together. The muscle in his cheek flexed twice before he said, "That's a good point, Samantha. A good observation. The criminal mind is not an easy one to decipher."

My mouth fell open. I slammed it shut. "Did you just compliment me?"

His lips twitched. "Yeah, but don't get too excited. Even a blind squirrel finds a nut sometimes."

I tossed my hand in the air in frustration. "And there you go, ruining the moment."

He smirked. "I gotta keep things real. Can't have you and Precious driving around playing Nancy Drew and Trixie Beldon."

I grimaced and cut my gaze to him. "Nancy Drew and Trixie Beldon? You couldn't come up with a more current comparison? Like Veronica Mars?"

"I'll stick with Trixie and Nancy."

"They aren't even in the same book? Or the same grade level of reading." Realization dawned. "Wait, is that what you're saying? One of us is smarter than the other?"

He barked a short laugh. "Maybe. Or maybe your first assumption was right, and I don't have a current reference. Deliberate? I'll let you decide." He cocked one brow, a half smile on his face. Then turned and strolled away.

"Wait." I caught up to him. "Do you need me to go take pictures of Smith's car for you?" Even if he said "no," I planned to follow him anyway. Ask for forgiveness later and all that.

He looped one thumb over his activity belt, casually holding the mug with his other hand, and kept walking. "That's not necessary. The staff photographer is available."

My phone jingled, and I tugged it from my pocket. Precious's name was on the screen. I stopped trying to keep pace with him and accepted the call.

"Looks like Nancy's calling. Or is she Trixie?" he called over his shoulder.

"I really don't like you," I said to his back, then put the phone to my ear. "What's up, P?"

"My car broke down. I need you to come and get me. I'm on Cougar Valley Road about three miles past Junkie's."

CHAPTER EIGHT

I found Precious leaning against her maroon Ford Focus, hood up. The ground around her was wet and in the air was a burnt smell.

The sun had penetrated the blanket of gray, and she had her face turned up to the sky. As a PNWer, you gotta get that vitamin D when you could. The sun was a fleeting treat in the fall and winter.

I pulled over to the shoulder across the lane from her and got out of LC. "What happened?"

Face still turned upward, she said, "I don't know. The check engine light came on, but I pushed it, hoping I'd make it to Bob's." She gestured to the hood. "Apparently not. Next thing I know, I hear a hissing sound and water is shooting out from the crack of the hood."

I looked at the engine. Her issue appeared to be the radiator. "Did you call Crenshaw?"

She nodded. "Right after I called you. He's finishing up a call but will be here as soon as he can."

I scanned the open field. Cougar Valley Road was nothing but country. At one end toward town was Junkie's and the main road that lead to downtown Wind River. In the direction Precious was coming from were farms, a handful at best. Since farming was becoming obsolete in the area, many were selling out to housing developments.

Precious's parents' farm was two miles down the road, I assumed she'd come from there. "How are your folks?"

"Doing well," she said. "I helped them set up the entrance to the corn maze and moved pumpkins into the barn to sell." She dusted imaginary dirt from her jeans. She didn't look like a woman who'd been farming, not dressed in a gauzy shirt with a four-inch-wide belt circling her waist.

In addition to running a restaurant, Precious's parents did the annual Halloween corn maze, pumpkin patch, and hayrides. They had apple orchards they turned into hard cider and kid-friendly cider, fields of gourds they used creatively, and a private vegetable and flower garden that could make the average backyard gardener weep with envy.

"Get this," I said. "Smith was being interrogated today when I went to the police station." Louney said I couldn't tell my dad. He didn't say I couldn't tell my best friend.

Precious pushed off the car, turned to me, stunned. "For robbing Junkie's and tying up Ms. Trina?"

I nodded. "Apparently, he was around here somewhere when they needed him to respond to Junior's accident with the deer, but they couldn't get him on the radio." I filled her in on the rest of what Leo told me.

She pointed to the field. "Sometimes when I leave mom and dad's late, a cop car is parked there. The interior is always dark, so I assumed whoever was in it was sleeping, but maybe Smith and Kevin meet out here. It's isolated and dark at night."

I considered the road. "And you can take back roads from here to Graycloud's place, too."

"You think these robberies are a copycat?" She crossed her arms and rubbed her hands up and down as if to warm herself.

"I do. Dad does. Louney does, or else why be talking to Smith and Kevin Greevey? If Louney believed the Comic Book Bandits were behind this, he'd be pursuing that, wouldn't he?" I had no real practical experience to pull from, so this was all guessing.

She nodded in agreement. "Recognizing that someone we know, someone we might have hung out with or dated or sat next to at the Fourth of July parade, is capable of doing terrible things to people is disturbing. It gives me the heebie-jeebies."

I leaned casually against her driver's side door. "It's not as if these people are serial killers. I don't think they meant for Ms. Trina to get hurt."

Precious reared back in horror. "Did you hear yourself? Who are you? Ms. Trina lost her arm. She wouldn't have been out there if whoever did this wasn't greedy and selfish. And stupid." She added emphasis to her last words.

Yikes, I was starting to sound like my dad. Leo's cautionary warning was ringing true. Exposure to the seedy side of life was changing my perspective, making me more casual about crime. And I'd been doing this two days. Not counting what we learned in school.

Not wanting to continue this conversation, I pointed over her shoulder. "Here comes Crenshaw."

She pushed me aside to reach into her car. Gathering her books, purse, and a water bottle, she then tossed them inside LC.

In silence, we watched Crenshaw pull up.

Before he got out of the tow truck's cab, I said, "You gonna ask about Bigfoot?"

Her eyes widened and she slapped her leg in frustration. "Darn it. I wish I'd thought about that. I wouldn't have called you and instead rode with him."

I chuckled. "Let's see if he'll tell us anymore."

Crenshaw jumped from the large cab and glanced between her car and us. "Where you want me to tow this? Bob's?" His lower lip jutted out from what I assumed was a plug of tobacco. A second later, he spat on the ground then wiped his chin with a bandana from his back pocket.

Precious shook her head. "I have to take it to Greevey's dealership. I called Bob, and he said it would take a week before he could get to it. I called Junior, and he can get to it tomorrow."

Crenshaw said, "Roger."

"Can we help?" I gestured to Precious's car.

"I got it," Crenshaw said.

I cleared my throat. "Becca was at the hospital. Ms. Trina wasn't awake while I was there. Have you heard how she's doing?"

Crenshaw nodded. "Yup, she's awake, but says she doesn't remember anything."

That surprised me. "Nothing?"

"Not even if Bigfoot came to the bar?" Precious asked.

Crenshaw chuckled. "Hard to imagine a person forgetting that. How did you know about that?"

Precious pointed to me.

"Because she loves Bigfoot," I said in my defense and cleared my throat from the guilt lodged there. I had been told to keep my lips zipped.

Precious sucked in a breath, her eyes wide with excitement. "Do you honestly think that's what was on the video?"

Crenshaw shuffled to the cab of his truck then came back to us holding a picture. "You tell me."

The image was grainy and black and white. The bottom left corner was a black blob, the bottom right showed the lower part of a leg, the foot not in the frame. The leg was hairy and built like a tree trunk, large and uniform in size from top to bottom. The backdrop for the leg was the junkyard.

"This looks as if the angle is coming from close to the ground and pointing up." I stared at the image.

Crenshaw cleared his throat in embarrassment. "It is. I thought I was being really clever putting a camera low to the ground. Everyone looks up for cameras, no one expects them to be down by the ground."

That made sense, to a degree. I pointed to the blob. "What's this?"

Crenshaw glanced at the picture then returned to hooking up the car. "Dirt on the lens. Trouble with low cameras is they get dirty faster. The elevated cameras had a film of dirt on them, but this one had mud splatters. I've since cleaned all my camera lenses."

Precious's face glowed with hope. She clutched the picture to her chest. "This could be the real deal. Can I keep this?"

Crenshaw's smile said he thought Precious was amusing. He nodded.

I was skeptical. "Or there could be another explanation. Anything else your videos might have caught? Like say, Officer Smith coming and going?"

Crenshaw was working at the hood of Precious's car, hooking up the wench. He stood and stared at me. "How did you know about that?"

Feeling like a busybody, I stuffed my hands in my pockets. "I went by the station earlier. He was there in the interrogation room."

Crenshaw shrugged. "I expect a lot of people will be seeing the inside of that interrogation room."

"How come?" This didn't make sense to me.

"Because the bar was packed that night. Someone had to see something. They probably don't know it yet." Crenshaw continued to hook up Precious's car.

"Seventies night is the best," I said.

"Biggest moneymaker for me." Crenshaw tightened chains and cables then moved to the tow truck to lift up Precious's car.

"And whoever did this had to know that." I was thinking out loud.

"What I can't figure out is why they went into the junkyard and what they took, if anything." Crenshaw said.

"Wait," I said. "You think the robbers took something from your junkyard, too?"

Crenshaw gave a half shrug. "That's my guess. Or else why go into the junkyard? I've got video of a figure moving through the yard, but they managed to stay far enough away from the camera to make out anything distinguishable."

"And the cameras were dirty," I guessed.

"That, too. The camera that caught the person was by the junkyard entrance. Not the same one that caught Bigfoot, which is closer to the back door of the bar."

Precious perked up.

I said, "I'm sure we can rule out Bigfoot. What do you think the person took?"

Crenshaw stroked his chin. "Anything worth

value would be car parts, but a part isn't as high value as an entire car."

I teased Precious. "Why would Bigfoot need car parts?"

Precious looked surprised. "Don't assume he wouldn't need car parts. Depending on what he took, he could use it for a lot of things. Like a hood could be a tabletop."

I smiled. "Because Bigfoot is domesticated and needs a table for sit-down dinners?"

She pointed a finger at me. "You tease, but one day when we find him and you see how he's living, you're gonna be blown away."

"I look forward to that day," I said.

The walkie-talkie on Crenshaw's hip crackled. He had another pickup to do following this one.

"Busy day?" I said after he'd written down the location of the broken-down vehicle.

"You ain't kidding. Now that word's out about cars getting stolen from dealerships like Greevey's, people want to be towed to a station that locks up their car or my junkyard behind the gate. People made fun of me for my cameras and gates, but no one is laughing now."

Precious said, "I don't have a choice with Greevey's. I need my car ASAP. Do you think I should go elsewhere? Do you know another body shop?"

Crenshaw and I shook our heads.

Precious sighed. "I'm gonna have to trust Greevey's."

Crenshaw worked the wad in his mouth then spit on the ground.

Precious continued, "Besides, who'd steal an old Ford like mine?" She looked heavenward. "Oh, please don't let it get stolen. I know my car isn't much, but it's all I have, and with midterms coming up, I can't be bothered to have to car shop if this one were to get stolen."

Confused and frustrated, I rubbed my temples. "But wasn't Junior's stolen because it's a sports car? Those are perfect to sell on the black market, right?" Like I knew anything about a market other than our town's farmer's market.

Crenshaw nodded and scratched at his cleanly shaved chin. "The parts, for sure. One of the main companies that makes the OEM's for those types of sports car recently had a fire in their factory, and now there's a backorder for all parts. Junior's lucky his car was stolen. It'll probably be easier to get a new car than get the replacement parts he needed."

"But he could use generic parts." Clearly, repairing cars was complex.

Crenshaw rolled his eyes. "Not Junior. Only the best for him."

This was the second person who said less than favorable comments about Junior, not counting his brother. My world was turning inside-out. What I believed to be true, wasn't. Who I believed to be nice might not be.

Crenshaw said, "You two have time to do me a favor? Or two favors?"

I looked at Precious, who shrugged as if to say why not. "Sure," I said.

He walked to the cab of the tow truck, then took out two large brown paper bags. "Can you deliver these bags to Becca? I've been meaning to get out there and see if she needs anything, but with all these calls coming in, I'm afraid the food will spoil before I get the chance."

I took the bags. "Yeah, we can totally do that."

Hopefully at Becca's I'd get answers, specifically about Kevin.

Crenshaw continued, "And can you spread the word that this Friday, Junkie's will be re-opening and we're having another seventies night fundraiser for Trina to help cover medical expenses and what not. You two will come, won't you?"

We both nodded.

I said, "I'll make sure to tell everyone I know."

He gave us a toothy smile. "Maybe Bigfoot will come back for tires to make himself some chairs to go with his hood dining table."

Precious clasped her hands together with excitement. "Oh, I sure hope so."

CHAPTER NINE

We drove to Becca's in silence. Precious was staring at the Bigfoot picture while inspecting it from different angles.

When we pulled up to Ms. Trina's, a rusted-out old sports car was parked in the driveway. Next to it was a Toyota Camry with a rental car sticker on its bumper.

"I hope we're not imposing," Precious said.

"We'll drop off the food and feel it out." I picked up the grocery bags and handed one to Precious, keeping the other.

The front door swung open before we could knock. A serious-looking man with sharp features stood before us. He was wearing a wrinkled suit and carried a briefcase.

"Excuse me." He didn't move, but gestured for us to get out of the way. He seemed irritated.

I stepped closer to Precious to allow him to

pass. He brushed by us and mumbled something that I hoped was an apology.

Becca was behind him. Her eyes were red and puffy from freshly shed tears.

"Is it your mom? Is she okay?" I was worried Ms. Trina wasn't out of the woods.

Becca dabbed a tissue to her eyes. "Every day goes from bad to worse." She waved us in.

We carried the bags to the kitchen and began to unload.

The Holland house was small but warm and cozy. The kitchen and dining combo was off the living room. A hallway led to the back of the house where I assumed were the bedrooms and bath.

"Is there anything we can help with?" I unpacked several packages of Oreos. Apparently, Crenshaw put stock in the belief that a cookie could fix anything.

Becca held a pack of cookies, confusion on her face.

"This is all from Crenshaw," I explained.

Becca collapsed in a chair and nodded. "That explains the Oreos. He knows they used to be my favorite."

Precious pointed to the front door behind her. "Who was that?"

Fresh tears sprung to Becca's eyes. "On top

of all this with mom, now I have to deal with Dad stuff, too."

I handed her a package of Double-Stuf. "Dad stuff?"

"That guy was a representative from Dad's company. Somehow they were never notified that Dad died." She took two cookies and fidgeted with them, twisting off the tops.

"Oh, dear," Precious said. "Like you want to be addressing this while your mom is in the hospital. Out of respect, his company should wait until you all are settled first."

Becca said, "Apparently, someone is using Dad's insurance agent authority and approving claims. His company thinks his identity was stolen."

"Holy cow." I helped myself to an Oreo. "I hope this doesn't make more of a mess for your mom to clean up. I read that companies can dedicate someone to handle this. Maybe your dad's company will take care of it for her. Your mom is gonna have her hands full." I gulped at my poor choice of words and hoped no one would notice.

The back door flung open and Kevin Greevey stepped into the kitchen. He shot Precious and me a glare. "Jeez, what are you two doing here."

I pointed to the groceries. "Crenshaw asked us to deliver groceries."

He pointed to the door. "You've done that. Now get out."

Becca sighed and asked him, "Did you find anything?"

He shook his head. "His office looks intact, and I couldn't get into the computer with any of the passwords you provided."

Becca said to me. "We thought maybe Dad's office was broken into, and that's how his identity might have been stolen. It's not like the barn has a secure front door."

Precious asked, "Your dad's office was in the barn?"

Becca nodded. "In a small room in the barn so not, like, out in the open."

Kevin continued to glare at me.

His angry-man-attitude was getting on my nerves. "What?" I said. "If someone told you they'd seen me fighting with Ms. Trina, would you have acted any different?"

"Kevin's used to being blamed for everything," Becca said.

I said to Kevin, "If it means anything, Bob thinks you're the smartest, bestest mechanic and restorer to ever grace his shop."

Precious said sotto voce, "He didn't use the word bestest, but he implied it."

Kevin ducked his head, running a hand over his face.

Becca said, "Kevin is the bestest. He's opened his own shop and has a wait-list of cars he's slotted to restore."

"Becs," Kevin said. "Remember we were keeping this quiet. We don't want my family to know."

"Our lips are sealed." Precious pretended to button her lips and mine.

At this rate, I was going to need superglue to keep my yap shut from spilling all the secrets I knew.

I gestured between the two of them, then pointed to Kevin. "Is that why you weren't with Becca on the ICU floor? You're hiding this from your family, too?"

Becca confirmed my guess with a nod.

"And you have your own shop?" I asked Kevin.

He crossed his arms. "Restoring classic and exotic cars."

I picked my next words carefully. Kevin was opening up, and I didn't want him to shut down again. "What do you think about your brother's car being stolen? Am I wrong to be surprised by this? Is it as common as others are telling me?"

Kevin shrugged. "Depends on the car. Junior's Saleen would be a hot item. And the tow truck driver he used has a shady reputation. Junior knows that. It makes me wonder if he picked him on purpose."

I said, "I do know Crenshaw was out of town. Maybe he didn't have a choice. "

Kevin snorted with disgust. "There is always a choice." He rubbed his fingers together in the sign for money. "My brother is a cheap bastard. That might have been the reason, too."

I wasn't sold. "I was there after he hit the deer. Junior was rattled. I'd buy him not thinking through the options."

Kevin rolled his eyes. "Junior always gets the benefit of the doubt, whereas I—"

Frustrated, I blurted out, "Don't help your cause. All we hear is about what your dad and brother tell us. You aren't out there fighting back." My points had merit.

Kevin wasn't having it. He gave a sharp, bitter laugh. "Because I have better things to do than worry about those two and their smoke and mirrors game. The further detached from them I am, the better off I'll be."

Becca said, "That's what he and my mom were fighting about Friday. She told him to stay away from me." She looked at Kevin and smiled sadly. "Us dating didn't bother her before. But I guess she thought we were getting more serious, so she forbade me to continue seeing him. She never gave me a reason."

Precious snorted. "As if that has ever worked on a kid anywhere."

Becca continued, "She threatened to throw me out, but she was bluffing. She can't afford to. I help with my sister, and Mom likes having me here. I told Kevin she was having a bad day and to let it cool off before he said anything to her." She directed her next remark at Kevin. "But sometimes his temper gets the best of him and he can't shut his mouth."

I said, "Bad day meaning just one of those days, or did something specific happen?"

"A few weeks ago, my Dad's company called, I answered, and they asked to speak to him. I lost it. I told them he was dead, and if their call was a prank, it was a cruel one. I accused them of making a sick joke and hung up on them. The next time they called, they got mom. The Friday the robbery happened at Junkie's, we found out Dad's company planned to hold us liable. Mom lost her mind."

Precious asked, "Liable for what?"

Becca shrugged. "Apparently, whoever stole his identity was collecting his paychecks, too. Dad's company opened an investigation." She pointed to the door. "That guy that was here is the one doing the investigating."

I said, "When they find the person who stole it, then they'll press charges and this drama can move on."

Becca burst into tears. Kevin rushed to her and wrapped her in a hug. Becca regained composure long enough to say, "Yeah, except they think my mom is the one who stole his identity."

CHAPTER TEN

After Becca's, Precious and I went back to my place. I scanned her Bigfoot photo into my computer, not because I wanted a possible Bigfoot image, but because I wanted a closer look.

Something about the hair on the legs bothered me. I was staring at the photo when Precious's phone rang.

Precious, having kicked off her shoes, was stretched out on my couch. She said, "Good, it's the service department."

The conversation had my full attention when she addressed Junior.

She rolled her eyes at me. "Yes, I understand. I need a new radiator, and my car will be ready in four days." She sighed. "Any chance you could speed that up?" Following a long pause, she then said, "Would it go faster if I bought a manufacturer's part?" She gave me a thumbs up. I guess she asked the question because of what we learned from Bob.

She gave me a look of disgust and pointed to the phone. "Well, if that's how it is." She sighed in defeat and hung up.

"What did he say?" I asked.

"That my car was a piece of crap."

"What?" I exclaimed. "Seriously?"

She flipped her hand in the air. "In a round-about way, he said it. When I asked if putting a manufacturer's part in my car would speed up the repair time, he actually laughed. Oh, he tried to cover it with a fake cough, but said that wouldn't be a good use of my money given the age of my car." She tossed her phone onto the couch. "Besides, he said something about the recent factory fire and assured me using a generic part would be faster and cheaper."

Because this was the second time the factory fire had been mentioned, I pulled the story up on the internet and scanned the article. I couldn't afford to spend energy on every word, so I looked for what I called speed bump words. Those were the essential words, not the filler words like *the* and *if*. In this case, the speed bump words were about the parts and the make and model of the cars involved.

I said, "Happened a week ago. The plant that

burned down made a variety of parts including radiators for Mustangs, Taurus, Focus, and Fusions." I tapped a pencil against my lip. "You need a radiator. Junior needed a radiator after he hit the deer. Which means no OEM for his high-end car."

She shrugged. "Maybe I should visualize mine getting stolen. It would be quicker to get a new car than wait for a repair."

I continued to tap. "No kidding. Especially when his dad owns the lot where he likes to shop. We should all be so lucky."

Precious stretched out on my couch. "Convenient. Though what a hassle. To deal with a stolen car would be huge. I'm sure the insurance company would be difficult."

None of the puzzle pieces were clicking together. "Your car is a straight-up repair. No insurance to bill. But had you had an accident, say…hit a deer, and you had a higher-end car, then Greevey's would be billing your insurance."

"And if my car were high-end, then I'd want OEMs, which cost more." After a pause Precious added, "And that raises my insurance premiums."

"But for Junior, that's not such a big deal because his shop does the repair, and I'm sure the markup is larger so Junior pockets that," I said.

Precious hummed in disagreement. "But one-time pocketing the extra from insurance isn't going to offset the monthly increase in the premiums."

"True, and you need permission from your insurance company to go with the higher-end parts. Bart Holland was the guy who approved OEMs, if I understand Becca correctly."

Precious said, "And Bart is dead, but someone is using his identity."

"Someone who is possibly making a lot of money if they are pocketing the difference." But even as I said it, I didn't buy it. Even if Junior was pocketing the difference, I doubted the amount was significant and too many other elements were out of Junior's control. Such as, who came into his shop and what insurance they carried.

"None of this makes sense," I said in frustration.

Precious sat up and slapped herself in the forehead. "I left all my notes for my midterm paper in my trunk."

"Good, we'll drive out to Greevey's, and maybe I'll get a chance to ask Junior about OEMs."

Before we headed out, I told Dad about what we learned. I also mentioned the pictures of each scene were currently up on my computer.

We drove the fifteen minutes to Greevey's in silence. Precious, ready for all this drama to be over, was in full visualization mode which, from the outside, looked like meditation and deep breathing.

It was as if the universe knew we were dense and required obvious signs because when we arrived, a customer was in the Parts and Services lobby screaming his head off at Junior. The customer was a meticulously dressed businessman with dark slicked-back hair and nails that shone as they caught the sunlight when he waved them furiously in Junior's face. Mr. Fastidious was practically foaming at the mouth from his anger.

"You said this would be done in a week, and now we're at the end of week three." Mr. Fastidious's index finger was half an inch from Junior's nose.

"There was a fire at the plant. The part was delayed, but one arrived Friday, and we're getting it prepped for your car."

"I've a good mind to yank my car and take it elsewhere. If my car isn't ready by Monday, I'll sue you. I'm sure I can find something negligent or illegal here." Mr. Fastidious gave a smile so wicked I was scared. He continued. "You've already given me plenty to use against you in court."

Junior stuck his hands in his pockets, an easy smile on his face. He looked chagrined. "Mistakes happen. We're rectifying it as best we can with the limitations we have."

This was the Junior I knew. Mr. Class President who got us a baked potato bar at the high school and cushioned chairs at study hall. He appeared sincere, his vibe trustworthy.

Mr. Fastidious' eyes narrowed. "Monday. No later."

Junior nodded. "Of course. That's what I said earlier. I appreciate your patience."

Mr. Fastidious stomped away, bumping Junior with his shoulder as he passed.

I followed him and, outside, I caught up with him. "Excuse me, sir. Do you have a moment?"

He spun toward me, his anger still in full flare. "What?"

"I…ah…um…" A ruse eluded me.

"You gonna spit it out or what? I don't have all day."

I went with the first thing to come to mind. "I saw what happened back there." I pointed to the parts office. "And my friend's car was towed here today, but now I'm worried she won't get quality service."

He scanned me up and down, his lower lip curled up. "I doubt you have much to worry about. I'm guessing your friend's car can be fixed with an old, used part. But I have a Shelby GT 500 with the Super Snake package. It's high-end."

He clearly thought I was dumb. I might not know what the Super Snake package was, and I didn't care. But it suited this guy, who was probably a super snake himself. "I'm guessing you want brand parts."

He huffed. "Nothing but the best. And that jackass in there pawns off generic parts."

I gasped in horror, which Mr. Fastidious seemed to appreciate. "How did you know?" Two pieces of the puzzle clicked together.

"I check up on this schmuck all the time. Came by one day last week and, sure as shit, the parts box was out by the car. Can you imagine?"

My eyes widened. "Lucky you came by."

He pointed his finger at me with a renewed sense of anger. "You're damn right, it is. The dumb broad who hit me, I had to fight her insurance company. They didn't want to pay. To go through all that and find this jackass not putting the brand part on was infuriating."

"I'm sure it was. But you have that guy nervous now." I pointed to Junior's office. "I think he'll do it right this time."

Mr. Fastidious snorted with derision. "All you ladies are gullible. That swindler will steal the coins from the bottom of your purse if he could. They all would." He glared back once for good measure then stormed off.

More pieces clicked together. I called Crenshaw and asked if he had a Shelby in his junkyard.

Precious came up behind me a few moments later. She had two notepads tucked in the crook of one arm. "I invited Junior to Junkie's on Friday."

"How did he respond?" I looked toward the parts department, seeking a visual on Junior, but he was nowhere to be found.

She shrugged nonchalantly. "At first he came up with a lame excuse."

That surprised me. If I was wrong, then he should have no reason to avoid Junkie's. If I was right, then my criminology class taught me it was not unusual for a criminal to revisit the scene of the crime.

I filled Precious in, connecting the dots with the information Mr. Fastidious had given me. We stared at each other, neither saying anything, she likely horrified by her thoughts like I was mine.

She said, "Do you think Junior did this to Ms. Trina because he's the one using Bart's ID?"

I shrugged, uncertain if we were making up farfetched ideas or on to something. "What if Ms. Trina found out about it and confronted him at the bar. He comes back after it's closed and…"

Precious made like she was dry-heaving.

"What?" I asked and steered her behind LC, away from where Junior might see.

She clapped her hands to her cheeks. "Junior insinuated that he wanted to get to know me better, and I flirted back. Ohmygawd. I flirted with a crazy person."

"I'm sure he won't be the last and, besides, we don't know if he's behind this. I'm only guessing. Speculating. Did you remind him the theme was seventies night again?"

She nodded.

I pulled my cell phone from my bag and called my dad. Precious and I were out of our element. We weren't cops. We weren't private investigators, and studying for the test didn't make me skilled. I took crime scene photos one time (two if you count the different scenes), so I was no expert. And Precious had quit her social worker courses to hone her life-coaching skills. Her goal? To help others get out of their head, visualize their success, and learn how to find strength in themselves for success. If Junior was our bad guy, he probably didn't need a life coach. After I filled Dad in on everything, he told me he would talk to Chief Louney.

I hung up, and we stared at each other in silence.

I said, "I don't think I can simply standby and wait."

"What are you thinking?"

I gave a casual shrug. "I think we chat him up Friday and see if we can trip him up or something. Maybe one of us can narrow down his timeline to see if it really is possible Junior did it."

Junkie's closed at two, and Junior called in his accident after four. In theory, he had plenty of time to get from one place to the other, but there were a lot of loose threads. Like Junior dressed for work and not heading away from Junkie's but toward it.

Precious ran her hands up and down her arms. "This entire situation gives me the creeps."

I couldn't agree more. "If we're right..." I couldn't finish the sentence. It was too awful.

Precious twirled a strand of hair nervously. "If we're wrong..."

I jerked open the car door. "I'd rather be wrong and considered a busybody or crazy person than right and not do anything about Junior. Especially if he's been swindling people, stole a dead man's ID, robbed Crenshaw and

Graycloud, and tied up a woman he's known all his life."

Precious sucked in a breath and blew it out slowly. "And hit that woman's car, which pushed it into her, and now she's lost part of her arm and hand."

I closed my eyes and recalled Junior's reaction when the call come across Rawlings and Leo's shoulder mic. "If all this is true, I think I can say with all honesty I don't believe Junior knew he hit her. He appeared as shocked as we did when the call came in."

The moment hung between us, and I was struck with a realization that left a bitter taste of betrayal in my mouth. "Unless that was a con, too. And if so, I don't know what to think about people anymore. About humanity."

CHAPTER ELEVEN

Friday came way too quick for my liking. Dad was doing research, trying to connect the dots. He had a poker game scheduled for the evening, and he would float everything by Chief Louney over cards and beer. I'm glad Precious and I made a separate plan as everyone else was moving too slowly for my liking.

Precious wore a bright blue polyester dress with giant abstract flowers in yellow and orange. Her skirt was so short she wore her old cheerleading tap pants underneath. White plastic knee-high boots capped off the outfit. Her hair was pushed back with a broad headband, a bouffant behind it. She looked groovy.

I'd gone with simple bell bottom pants set in earth tone stripes and platform shoes. I curled my hair and let it hang loose in fat loops. Pepper spray was tucked in my pocket, just in case. My camera was in LC for the same reason. Though I was confident I didn't want to use either one.

It was late evening by the time we arrived. Junkie's was hopping. A banner stating the cause was strung across the bar, and Becca was making thank-you rounds to a full house. Disco music pulsed through the space while Crenshaw and a female lumberjack-looking woman named Lindy—I was guessing his lady friend from Seattle—were working the bar.

From here, I had no backup plan. The original was to get Junior to talk. Maybe he'd trip himself up. But with the music, talking was too hard. And Junior wasn't acting odd. Not like I imagined a person who was doing bad things would act. But maybe he was seasoned and didn't blink twice at committing a crime.

Or maybe I was all wrong with my suspicions. But that was unlikely. Particularly when Crenshaw told me he did have a 2008 Shelby GT with the backend missing in the junkyard. He couldn't definitively say the side panel was stolen, but it definitely wasn't on the car in the yard.

The closer we got to closing time, the more the crowd thinned.

Junior had Precious cornered by the hors d'oeuvres table. He fit the seventies bill with his blond hair feathered back, his white shirt open to the belly button, and heavy gold chains around his neck. His pants were plaid and tucked into black shag boots. Parts of the faux goat fur were matted. *Blech,* Junior's taste was gross.

I made my way to them. This entire idea of trying to trap him was a bust. Leaving was my newest priority.

"Hey," I shouted over the music. "Sorry to interrupt, but I'm getting a headache. Are you ready?" I asked Precious.

"Yes," she said with a bright smile. "The night was a lot of fun. Thanks, Junior, for all the company." She looked at me. "Did you know Junior got those boots in Italy when he went last year to visit the Lamborghini factory?"

Junior faced me, his thumb looped under his necklaces. "These, too, gold is dirt cheap there."

"Good to know," I shouted.

A second later, three men stormed into the bar. One jerked the jukebox plug from the wall, creating instant silence. The disco ball continued to spin.

The newcomers were dressed in all black except each one sported a superhero mask and carried a really big gun. So big they hung the guns from straps running across their bodies.

"Everyone get down on the ground," Batman shouted as he waved his gun in the air.

The Hulk ushered Crenshaw and Lindy from around the bar to where the rest of us had gathered.

"I said down," Batman roared. "Hands behind your heads."

We all dropped to the floor and did as he demanded, me between Precious and Junior. Crenshaw was to the far left of us. To my right were three guys I didn't know as they'd been more than four years ahead of me in school.

"Nobody do anything stupid, and everyone will be okay," Batman said. He strolled between us. "We're here for the money."

"And to set the record straight," Iron Man said as he guarded the door. "Some poser is pretending to be us and making us look bad."

The Hulk was behind the counter, putting money into a pillowcase.

"That poser might be B-B-Bigfoot," Precious said.

No one moved for a beat. I groaned. When Precious got nervous she babbled and stuttered.

"What did you say?" Iron Man asked her.

"Some people think it was B—Bigfoot that robbed this place last week." She looked up, hands still clasped behind her head. "I was kinda h-h—hoping that was true."

A few muffled laughs from behind masks. Batman continued to pace. On his third lap, he stopped in front of Junior. "Stand up," he said and pointed his gun at Junior.

Junior stood. Batman gestured to Junior's boots and looked at Iron Man.

Iron Man said as he approached, "Dude, did you even see yourself in a mirror before you left the house to come here?"

Junior said. "It's seventies night."

Iron Man pointed to Junior's boots. "And what are those?" He pointed his gun at Precious. "This your girl? You wear those boots because she has a Bigfoot fetish?" Iron Man snorted. "She's a looker, but I wouldn't wear those boots for any chick."

I cut my gaze to the side to look at Junior's boots. The flash of the disco ball was light enough that it cast a shadow in such a way the shag, at this angle, looked like hair. An epiphany exploded in my head. No confession from Junior needed. I had the confirmation I'd been seeking.

I rolled to my side, careful to keep my hands on the back of my head and said to Junior. "How dare you? Shame on you."

Iron Man looked between Junior and me. "What? Is this your girl? Did I just get you busted, man with the girl boots?"

"No," I said. "He's the guy who impersonated you all last week and robbed this place."

"Shut up, Samantha," Junior shot me a look of annoyance.

It reminded me of the same look teachers would give me when I couldn't read the text they wanted.

"What?" Iron Man and Crenshaw said at the same time.

Disgusted, I said, "The boots. Look at the boots. Given the black and white of the video camera, the dirt on the lens, the wind that night, and the angle of the camera, Junior's boots look like hairy legs."

With disappointment, Precious said, "Aw, man. I really wanted Bigfoot."

I said, "Junior stole the car part off the Shelby because he knew his customer could and would make trouble for him. He got caught trying to put generic parts on the guy's car when he was charging him for OEMs."

"Original Equipment Manufacturer. It's the brand part for the car," Precious told the room.

Batman joined Iron Man.

"That's not true," Junior said dismissively. "She's making all that up." He circled his finger around his head in the universal sign for crazy.

I seethed. "You caught Ms. Trina at closing. You robbed the place to cover your tracks because what you were actually after was the car part. In addition, you've been using Bart Holland's identification and approving OEM parts for cars that customers didn't ask for, aren't you? And you're keeping the money. But why rob this place? Why not wait until Ms. Trina left for home?" By this time, I had the room's attention.

Crenshaw said, "Because the cameras outside point at the junkyard entrances and slightly beyond. But"—he pointed to a door at the back of the bar— "that goes to the junkyard and there isn't a camera posted there. I have a few out back that are aimed at the junkyard but the coverage is patchy. It's easy to move around back there and not get caught on camera. But to get out of the junkyard and not be seen he needed to come back through *that* door." He jabbed his finger toward the door for added emphasis.

Junior's expression was a mask of calm, but from my position on the floor I watched him repeatedly clench his fists.

Iron Man said to Junior, "You dirty bastard. Why would you steal from where you live? Rule number one—don't shit where you eat."

"Or sleep," Batman said.

Junior leaned toward the masked criminals and said in a stage whisper, "I'm telling ya, she's a nutter. Not too bright if you know what I mean."

He cut me a look full of menace.

But I was no quitter.

Junior hadn't done this alone, and that elusive bit of information was eating at me. "Who helped you? Was it a mechanic from the shop? You didn't do this alone. Two people held up Graycloud's diner. Two people had to do this job, too. You couldn't have carried that part out by yourself."

Junior kicked at me, but was stopped by Batman from taking a second swing. "You think you're so smart, but you don't know anything." He faced the superheroes before him, and like flipping a switch, went into full charm mode. The sort that one man used on another when trying to say they had stuff in common. "I apologize for using you all as a cover, but hopefully you understand. The opportunity was too great to pass up, and I essentially killed two birds with one stone."

"You're awful," I said. "Ms. Trina lost her arm because of what you did."

The Hulk came from around the bar and held up the pillowcase. "We're set. Let's blow this joint."

"Cut me loose from this," Junior said. "I need

a head start from the cops. You get what I'm saying."

Iron Man said, "You think you're like us?"

Junior shrugged. "We're both entrepreneurs. Am I right?"

Batman tossed a few plastic novelty rings on the floor. A comic book page floated down and landed on the floor a foot away from me. Just as dad had said.

Iron Man said, "Dude, this is our deal. Our MO. You made us look bad. Clumsy. I'm not feeling benevolent."

To the superheroes, Junior said. "I can make it worth your while." He jangled his necklaces.

Crenshaw said, "Excuse me, Comic Book Bandit fellas, but I'm the owner of this establishment. Trina was not only my friend, but my employee. If you aren't feeling so benevolent toward him, then maybe you might feel a little for the man who's been robbed twice in two weeks. Leave Junior behind and let me deal with him. I got a set of chains in the back of my pickup out there that have his name on them."

Junior let his necklaces fall through his fingers. "I'll give you all of these to start."

I said, "He told me he got those in Italy dirt cheap. I bet they're fake. Was the deer fake, too? How did you manage to make it look like the deer hit your car?"

Junior bit out a laugh. "Coincidence. Or bad luck. Depends on how one wants to look at it. Had I waited to leave for work at my normal time, I'd have never hit that deer. But I turned that luck around when I had my car stolen. So, you can't prove any of this. There's no evidence against me, and I'll be long gone before these Mayberry cops decide to question me."

It was my turn to give a snarky laugh. "You'll get caught. You know how I know that? You're sloppy." I pointed to the three guys in masks. "These guys. They're not sloppy. Chief Louney knew by the scene at Graycloud's diner we were dealing with a copycat. Here, too. Even my dad knew this was a copycat deal, and he's just waiting for the okay before he goes public with it. It was only a matter of time before they figured you out."

Batman moved to stand before me. His gun down by his leg. "Who's your dad?"

"He owns the local paper. He's a reporter."

From behind the plastic mouth of Batman's mask, the guy smiled. "Excellent."

I turned my attention back to Junior. "And if Chief Louney can't put the pieces together, you know my dad can. He brought the football league to their knees; no two-bit auto parts conman will outwit him. You go ahead and run, Junior, but you'll spend half the time looking over your shoulder." Anger was flowing through me. Anger for Ms. Trina and Becca and all they'd lost and suffered. "And Ms. Trina will have her day in court, and she'll see you pay for all you've done."

Junior laughed, tossed his head back and busted out a deep hearty laugh. He settled a moment later and stared at me with dark, soulless eyes. "Who do you think my partner was? Huh? Some guy we went to high school with? Nope, it was the squeaky-clean lunch lady, Ms. Trina herself."

The perception of my world and the people in it exploded as my brain processed what he said. Gone was the naivete that came with being ignorant to the seedier side of life. This wasn't a made-up TV show. People I knew and trusted had shown their true colors. I desperately wanted Junior to be a liar.

"Dawg, that's off the chain!" the Hulk said. "This pillowcase of money was a fundraiser for this Ms. Trina, and gold chains and furry boots here is saying she was his accomplice." He gave a short laugh. "That's priceless. Guess I don't feel so bad taking her money now."

Batman stared at Junior. "You left a man behind. A wounded man? Or woman in this case."

"He wounded her," I pointed out. "He was in such a hurry to get away, he hit her car, and the force pushed her car into her hand. Could've killed her."

Junior shrugged. "I did what I had to do."

Batman said, "Tie them up. Except for Junior here. He's coming with us."

CHAPTER TWELVE

They tied us up in pairs. My back was to Precious's, our hands behind us so that they touched. Crenshaw and Lindy were tied up, and one of the three dudes was hogtied since he was the odd number. They'd blind-folded us and, I was guessing, turned out the lights because everything was dark. The only flashes of light I could make out from behind the cloth covering my eyes were flashes of blue, green, and red. The disco ball.

Then, as if being held up and finding out Ms. Trina might have been Junior's accomplice wasn't horrible enough, the Comic Book Bandits raised the fear level one more notch. They turned on what sounded like an old-fashioned egg timer. Told us to not move until the timer dinged. Or else.

The tick tick of the timer was unnerving.

What if it was more than an egg timer? What if it was connected to something, like those sticks of dynamite Wile E. Coyote always found himself faced with? Dad hadn't mentioned this tidbit. Since no other place they'd robbed exploded, I could assume we'd be safe. But…

No way was I gonna hang around and find out. Criminals escalated. That was a known fact and always talked about on true crime shows. They'd been mad that Junior was bringing down their reputation. Maybe that pushed them over the edge.

"I'm really glad I wore these tap pants," Precious said. "Or else I'd feel exposed."

"Not that anyone can see," I reminded her.

I'd asked her to try to stand with me. Currently, we were both in a weird squat position, pushing against each other for leverage. But the task was hard as gravity kept trying to pull us to the side so we were constantly listing and correcting.

That, and my stupid shoes were sliding on the floor.

She said, "What if someone is in the room watching us? They can see."

"Then I'm sure they'd have busted a gut by now." We'd fallen twice on our side and had writhed like a fish out of water for a good five minutes before we were able to sit up.

"My thighs are burning," she said.

Mine were on fire. Connected as we were, her trembles flowed through me.

I sucked in a deep breath and blew it out. "Ready? On three. One. Two. Three."

We pushed and strained, constantly adjusting.

"What do you blind birds plan to do once you're up?" one of the dudes asked.

Precious and I teetered and overcorrected, resulting in our heads knocking. We cried out simultaneously, but kept trying to straighten. Finally, we were standing.

"We're up, right?" she asked.

"I think so. Feels like it," I said. The rope was slack, like it could fall off us, but wasn't. "What's the rope hung up on?" I said.

Precious groaned. "This position with my hands behind my back pulls my shoulders back and my... you-know-what forward." She cleared her throat.

"The rope is stuck on your boobs?" I was incredulous.

Her voice was low. "It would seem so."

I laughed. Hard. Until tears streamed down my face. Precious had embraced her abundant chest size the minute she got attention for them in junior high. She'd never complained when cheering or having to run at PE. She was always a glass half full person.

I finally settled. "I never thought I'd see the day where your chest would keep us from freedom. If that ticker goes off and is followed by something awful, we're gonna be dead because your boobs killed us." I snort-laughed.

"It's not funny," she said.

"It's really funny," I said. "At this moment, I'm thankful for my handful-sized ones. I'll never bad-mouth them again."

She sighed. "I have an idea, but I think you'll hate it."

"Hit me with it. What do we have to lose?" It was weird having a conversation with her, our backs to each other, and nothing but flashes of random light.

Precious said. "Remember in cheer when we'd stunt and I'd flip someone over my back?"

"No."

She huffed in frustration and stomped a foot. "What do you mean no? What were you watching at all those games?"

I stiffened. "Not you! I was busy watching my baton, hoping to catch it and not hit anyone with it." Being a majorette had been an insanely stressful time.

Precious's tone was heavy with annoyance.

"After the majorette program was canceled, what did you watch?"

"The football players and the game," I said. "Duh. Get on with this. What's your plan?"

A silent moment passed. Precious was probably sulking. "We'll probably end up on the floor again."

"What's the plan?" I said between clenched teeth.

"Oh, fine already. I was thinking, I'll lean forward, you on my back, and shimmy the rope down."

My mind's eye refused to create this image. "You think you can shimmy with me on your back?"

"I knew you wouldn't like it."

"Can't you suck them in?" Yep, we were going to end up on the floor again.

"I'd like to see this," one of the guys said.

Precious said, "They aren't inflatable or deflatable. I can't let air out of them."

"How awesome would that be?" another guy said, and he and his friends began to laugh. "Gives a whole new meaning to fun bags."

"Shut up," Precious and I said in unison.

Tick, tick, tick.

Crenshaw said, "Girls, focus. Try something. Try anything."

I tapped her with my hands. "Okay. Count it down so I'm ready."

We both took big breaths.

"Visualize this working," she said.

"I'll visualize not falling on my head," I mumbled.

"Three. Two. One."

She eased me into a hands-free backbend. Slow and steady. Our balance was precarious with our hands behind us. I impersonated a noodle. Limp.

"Now comes the hard part," she panted.

"Wait, roll your shoulders in first. Try that." The rope had shifted down slightly, and I was hoping to avoid the shimmy.

When her shoulders rolled, the ropes around me tightened across my middle, then slid down a tad.

Precious made a quiet gasp. "Here's the plan. I'll stand up quickly. I think when I do, the straps will fall. They're right at the...er...tips."

"I'm ready," I said.

Seconds later, I was moving through the air, propelled forward. Instinct had me wanting to put out my hands, but I couldn't. The rope slipped more, and as my nose went over my toes, the ropes slipped down to the ground.

My next problem was my forward trajectory

as momentum pushed me blindly ahead into parts unknown.

Apparently, the rope had pooled, and my foot got caught up in the coils, tripping me up. Afraid I would head dive into the floor, I twisted at the last second and landed on my left side.

SNAP!

The sound echoed across the room.

I yelped in pain.

Crenshaw asked. "What was that?"

I groaned. "Me falling. And I think I broke my collar bone." The awkward angle of the bone, a portion poking up toward my face, assured me my assessment was bang on.

"Sam, what should I do now?" Precious asked.

We were free from each other, but our hands were still tied and our blindfolds on. I gritted my teeth through a wave of pain, then said, "Can you find me? Maybe if you come up behind me, I can get your blindfold off." Standing wasn't an option. Pain shot through my side and killed any desire to move.

"Okay," she said. "Marco?"

"Polo," I said, my voice trembling.

Precious shuffled toward me as we played the game. When she found me by accidentally kicking my leg, I cried out in pain. My whole body was humming in agony.

"Be careful," I said. "The pain is off the hook."

She rustled around me like a dog trying to find a hidden treat. My fingers got tangled in her hair as I searched for the blindfold material, but every time I clenched my fingers, a burst of pain would shoot up my arm. Eventually, I was able to work it off.

"Oh, thank heavens," Precious said.

"Is it off?" Crenshaw asked.

"Yes," Precious said.

Moments later, her hands tickled my face, and then the blindfold came off. She came around and smiled at me, her teeth gleaming in the spinning disco light.

"The ticker," I said.

Like a baby giraffe, she stood and searched for the timer. "It's not connected to anything. It's a regular egg timer."

A collective sigh came from all of us. Next Precious turned off the disco ball and on the lights. Life was beginning to feel…hopeful. First, I wanted all of us to be safe. I'd worry about Junior and his accusations later. It was hard to believe Ms. Trina might be involved. What makes a person take a sideways turn and go bad?

With her hands still tied, Precious went about removing everyone's blindfolds.

Crenshaw said, "Call the police, Precious. On the cordless under the counter, all you need to do is press the ON button and one. That's speed dial for nine-one-one."

Precious made the call and requested an ambulance. There were tears in her voice. We all were probably teared up with relief. Fat, wet blobs coursed down my face.

Precious came to me, her face stained with tears, her black mascara smudged. "Are you okay? Should I move you?"

"No," I said. "Can you open the door? It's stuffy in here." Pain was making me lightheaded.

Precious opened the door to the outside then gasped. "Junior is out here chained to a pole. He has a sign hanging from his neck that says, 'This coward left a man behind' *and* he's naked."

CHAPTER THIRTEEN

The bed in the ambulance was beyond comfortable, or perhaps it was the painkiller being intravenously infused into me that was making me chillaxed.

Outside the rig, Chief Louney was telling his staff what to do. Boyd Bartell, the usual crime scene photographer, was methodically taking pictures between wiping his forehead with a handkerchief. Several large Paladin lights were set up around the perimeter, making the scene bright as daylight.

Junior hadn't been unchained as of yet, but he'd stopped proclaiming his innocence when Crenshaw bent low and whispered something in his ear. Dad was milling about interviewing people.

Precious climbed into the rig and sat on the bench beside my bed.

She said, "I'm sorry."

I was staring at my fingers, marveling at how they blurred when I moved them. "For what?"

"For your collar bone breaking. It was my idea that led to this." She waved her hand over my arm in the sling.

"We're free because of your idea." I showed her the hand on my non-injured arm. "Watch. When I move them really fast, they blur." I opened and closed my fingers. "Cool, right?"

She giggled. "Um, I think they only blur for you."

My eyes widened. "You think? That's cool."

"I think it's the medicine they gave you."

"Oh," I said, pointing outside the ambulance. "They're moving Junior." Leo was helping Junior to stand. He draped a blanket around him.

I said, "That's a relief. I *did not* want to see his butt."

Precious snorted. "Or anything from the front."

"That, too." It was then I noticed Junior was still wearing his boots. "I'm sorry your Bigfoot turned out to be that dumb-dumb." I pointed in Junior's direction.

Precious sighed. "Me, too."

"Maybe you should think about connecting

with a group of like-minded, er…fans." The idea had come from nowhere but sounded good to me. Based on the expression on Precious's face, she liked it, too.

"I might just do that." She gently touched the sling. "You aren't mad at me, right?"

I slouched back against the propped-up bed and smiled. "Nope."

"Hey, Sammy," Dad said, standing outside the ambulance. "How's my girl?"

"Feeling good, Daddy-o."

Dad chuckled. "The meds kick in, did they? Not feeling any pain?"

"Oh, my shoulder is killing me, but these meds make me not care. It's glorious."

Dad said, "Your mother is worried. She'll meet us at the hospital as soon as you give the driver the okay to leave."

I shook my head. "Can't leave until I know the truth." I dropped my voice to a whisper. "Junior said awful things about Ms. Trina. I don't think any of it's true."

Dad stepped into the back and sat on the bench next to Precious. "I'm sorry to say it's likely true." Dad briefly ducked his head and sighed. When he looked up, he looked sad. Or maybe disappointed.

"At poker tonight… Jeez, I guess last night

since it's now three in the morning. Louney confided Bart Holland's employer, AllCover Insurance, had contacted him about identity theft and possible money laundering. He sent Rawlings to question Trina. She's not singing like a canary yet, but with what she did say and what we've found out here, this is what we think happened." He wiped a hand down his face before he continued.

"According to Trina, Bart Holland died without life insurance. With Becca in college and the other soon to follow, she was desperate for money, and the extra jobs she took weren't covering it. Shortly after Bart's funeral, Junior approached Trina with a proposition. To use Bart's signature and approval to run these auto part scams. Apparently, Junior had been doing it on a small scale, but if he could bring in an agent to carte blanche approve repairs for OEMs, then he'd make even more. He offered to split that with Trina."

I squeezed my eyes shut. Thankfully, the drugs in my system dulled the ache of my disappointment with Ms. Trina's involvement.

Precious said, "But how did they get around his employer not finding out about his death?"

"Trina hadn't told them. His death was unexpected, and everything following happened fast. Because his company's headquarters is in a different state, she impersonated him in emails to continue to collect his checks and the kick-backs from Junior's scam."

I opened my eyes and brought my dad into focus. "And Graycloud's diner?"

"Apparently, Bart's company wasn't happy with all the approvals Trina was doing on behalf of his name. They called to speak with him, and Becca told them he was dead."

"Ah-ha," I said and went to snap. I had three thumbs and three middle fingers, and trying to figure out which lined up with the other one was hard. "When she told her mom about the call, Ms. Trina flipped out."

Dad nodded.

Precious squinted in confusion. "But I don't get what that has to do with robbing Junkie's or Graycloud's."

"Me either," I said then laughed.

Dad shrugged. "Couple of motivators, I suppose. Trina said something about paying back Bart's company for the wages they paid out since his death. But also, Junior was in trouble with a few customers down at the shop. One guy was bringing in an inspector for confirmation that the parts were OEMs. With the fire at the manufacturer, Junior couldn't get the parts he needed and had told him was on the car. He needed to break into the junkyard and take parts from here."

"What are the odds Crenshaw would have the part?" Precious asked.

Dad nodded. "Exactly. Junior was one lucky son of a gun. But I'm sure if he couldn't get what he needed from Crenshaw, he'd have found another place to rob. Desperation does that to people. This inspector could blow everything wide open."

Leo came around the corner and surveyed us before asking Dad, "You giving them the run down?"

Dad nodded.

I said, "He admitted hitting the deer was a coincidence."

Leo said, "But getting his car stolen wasn't. He planned that." Leo climbed into the rig and lowered to his haunches at the foot of my bed. "That picture you took of Trina's car showed red paint from hers and from another. We had that analyzed, and it matched the same color on his Saleen. My guess is he didn't want to take any chances and made the car disappear."

"And Jeff Smith?" I remember the officer crying in the interrogation room.

Leo answered. "Had nothing to do with it.

Was sleeping in a field out on Cougar Valley Road. Had his radio turned low."

I clasped the hand from my uninjured side over my eyes as the truth sunk in. People I knew. People I'd trusted on face value had been lying and conning me and others for a while now. Whatever their reason didn't matter. "I think I'm ready to go to the hospital, Dad."

"Okay, princess," he said. His lips brushed across my forehead.

I peeked from under my palm, both Dad and Precious were getting out of the ambulance. Leo was staring at me.

"What?" I let my hand fall to my side.

"It's one thing to discover people you like are crooks. But in the span of one week, you've broken a collar bone, been tied up, robbed, and emptied your stomach contents on what we know now is part of a second crime scene. That's a full week for you." He arched one brow. "I spread a lot of what you've experienced over time. Not you, though, you come in and rip the Band-Aid right off."

"I'm courageous like that," I said, my words slurring slightly. The pain in my shoulder had moved into a dull ache, and my high was making me sleepy.

"Are you drunk?" A hint of laughter edged his voice.

I was horrified by his question. "What? I was given a pain killer."

His look was skeptical. "First the flu, now a pain killer. Sounds like excuses." He fake-coughed into his hand.

"I think you should go away. Shoo." I waved my hand like I was swatting at an annoying insect.

He moved to the bench and put his hand over mine. "Think long and hard about this career path, Samantha. Is this what you want your days to be like? I think you should take pictures of babies dressed as peapods, instead. Stick to the bright side."

I wasn't sure I wanted to see this dark side of people on a regular basis, either, but I didn't want to talk about it right now. "Ew," I said. "Your hand is sweaty. Gross." I slid my hand away.

"I'm serious, Samantha" he said.

"Me, too. You should see a doctor about your excessive sweatiness." When I listed in his direction, he pushed me back upright.

I continued, "It would seem this line of work bothers you as well, Leo. Maybe *you* should check *your gut*, too." I attempted a snide snarl, but my lips were numb and not working. The effort alone cracked me up. I pinched my lips between my fingers twice before letting go. "I can't feel them."

"I figured that out," he said. "I'm trying to be serious here. Maybe this isn't the best time."

I pinched my lips once again, let go, then said, "Puh-shaw." I waved a dismissive hand in his direction. "There would never be a better time to be honest. Here's the thing, Leo. All my life I've been poor little Samantha True, the girl who couldn't learn to read. And if you want to know what that might be like, ask your brother." I closed my eyes and blew out a deep sigh. "Maybe Hue was right to leave town and start over someplace where a stigma wasn't attached to him. Taking these pictures was important to me. I was going to be good at something, at this. What does it say if I walk away? Everyone will wonder if I'll ever amount to anything."

His brow furrowed. "People will know you helped solve this case. They'll know you did a good job."

"Perfect, I did a great job and still walked away, but what does that say? Do I become a one hit wonder? Like that song from your past you really love but you can't think of anything else by that band? I'll be like that. And never mind the report you and Rawlings submitted to my professor was less than stellar."

He wiped a hand down his face. "There's that."

I didn't dare look at him for fear I'd see pity in his eyes. Instead, I pointed to the door. "Time for you to get lost. I want to enjoy the last bits of this high before I fall asleep, and your presence is ruining that."

Always the single-minded guy, he said, "You'll think about what I said? I'd hate to see this job change you for the worse. Who cares what people say about you if you aren't happy with the choices you've made? That's what really counts."

"Blah, blah, blah. That's what I hear when you talk." I let my lids close to block out the sight of him.

Trouble was, he was right. In my dreams, the bad guys looked like people I knew. I didn't want to always see the bad side of people. I wanted light and happiness. More than I wanted this achievement, to make my parents proud with my college degree, I wanted to be happy. Life had been hard enough already.

And that's why I decided Leo was right. I would be better off taking pictures that didn't leave dark, lasting impressions. But I'd never admit that to him in this lifetime.

SAMANTHA'S STORY continues in the next book in this series called ALL BETS ARE OFF. Fast forward 10 years and Samantha's life is upside down and she's once again forced to deal with the seedier side of life. Turn the page to read the first few chapters of ALL BETS ARE OFF.

STERY ·

**PI means
e is steep.**

g with the gang.
unit first.

RISTI ROSE

LL BETS
ARE OFF

RISTI ROSE

AUGHT OFF
GUARD

LOOKING FOR MORE SAMANTHA TRUE?

ALL BETS ARE OFF

FOR FANS OF VERONICA MARS!

Some days, no matter how awful, are not worth a do-over

During a wild weekend in Vegas Samantha True and her boyfriend impulsively marry. Six months later she learns three things about her new husband.

1. He's been killed in a freak accident.
2. She's inherited his secret PI business.
3. He had another wife.

Broke and devastated, she dives into learning the PI business—how hard can it be? Following a binge-watching How To session on Youtube, Samantha's ready to take her first case.

When mysterious strangers show up at her

doorstep demanding information about her dead husband, she realizes she's in over her head.

Samantha must discover who her husband really was. Yet, what if the truth puts her in danger, too?

CHAPTER 1
FRIDAY

"Miss True, I have some very troubling news." The lawyer, Tyson Lockett, pushed a tri-folded piece of paper across the desk toward me.

The corner hung off the side of the desk.

Wishing I could avoid the paper all together, I flicked it back toward him using the nail of my index finger. After which, I rubbed the finger down the length of my skirt, wiping it clean.

His expression solemn, he said, "I have more troubling information."

"More troubling news than my husband's been killed?" I swallowed hard; those had been difficult words to say.

What could trump learning of your loved one's unexpected death? My mind couldn't conceive of one thing.

Lockett wiped a hand down his face and mumbled something that sounded like he was cursing the dead man in question.

He pinched the bridge of his nose and said without looking at me, "I'm not sure how to tell you this, Miss. True. If you look at the death certificate, you'll see that the name and date of birth align with the man you knew as Carson Holmes. But if you look closer, you'll notice the cause of death, nature of death, and date of death are wrong." Then he fixed his gaze on me. His stare unwavering.

I shook my head. "I don't think I understand." My mouth was insanely dry and rough, like sunbaked earth. Nothing about this moment added up. I locked onto the easiest of oddities coming at me. Lockett knew to call me and tell me about Carson, though I'd never heard the lawyer's name before today. Lockett also knew I had kept my maiden name. "How did you know I hadn't taken Carson's last name?"

He blew out a heavy sigh then nodded to the paper. "Please take a look at this." Lockett leaned across his steel and glass desk and nudged the folded piece of paper, perfect for a letter-sized envelope, back to me.

With trepidation, I reached for the document. My hand trembled slightly as I picked it up by pinching the corner with my thumb and forefinger.

The sheet had weight, the sort of paper used for official documents or homemade cards declaring love or good news.

Lockett gave me an encouraging half smile and nod, silently pushing me to keep going.

I clutched the heavy paper, one hand on each side, and lifted the top with my thumbs. The inside print declared the sheet to be an official death certificate from Washington State.

"I know this isn't easy and I'm very sorry," he murmured calmly.

Something about his downturned gaze gave me the impression that he was saddened by the news, too. Or maybe he was sad because he was charged with delivering it.

He cleared his throat. "Two nights ago, the man you knew as Carson Holmes was killed in a motor vehicle accident. He was driving through Snoqualmie Pass, crashed, and a tree fell onto his car."

My mind played its own version of the scene just painted for me. "Impossible," I whispered. I directed my focus on the lawyer as I expelled a deep breath. "Carson was in California at a home security convention, not northern Washington, and certainly not anywhere near the pass."

How did I know this guy was even telling me the truth? Yesterday, I had no idea he existed, and today he was lowering this boom.

"Why aren't the police telling me this if Carson is really dead?" I closed my eyes, seeking equilibrium, and rewound the last few moments. "Why did you keep saying the man I knew as Carson Holmes?"

"Look at the certificate," Lockett said. "Look at the date and cause of death."

With steely resolve, I opened my eyes and further unfolded the paper. I scanned the page for the important words like "nature of death" and skipped the rest. Lockett was correct; the date of death was not today or yesterday or the day before. The date was from ten years ago and on New Year's day. Today was not New Year's or anywhere close to it. The cause of death confused me more. "This says Carson Holmes died from cancer."

"That's correct," Lockett said.

"So this isn't my husband?" A tiny spark of hope pulsed inside, even if I couldn't figure out this riddle.

"No. Your husband used that death certificate to establish a new identity. The man you knew as Carson Holmes was not really Carson Holmes."

"Come again?" I wasn't usually this dense, but nothing this lawyer had said made a lick of sense, starting with his anxious phone call this morning.

"The man you believed you were married to had a different name, a different birthday, and was actually married to another woman. Well, they were in the final stages of divorce, but that doesn't matter. What does is that it wasn't official yet."

And there it was, the *other* bad news. Yes, death was still the worse of the two, but learning my husband was actually married to someone else ranked up there really close to learning he'd died.

The words came to me as if Tyson Lockett was standing at the far end of the tunnel, his voice metallic and fading. His words tasted bitter on my tongue even though I hadn't spoken them.

I had one of two options. I could toss my cookies onto his shag gray carpet or I could pass out.

Neither sounded appealing, but I chose the latter. And considering how my luck was going, I took preemptive measure and stuck my head between my legs. Didn't want to faint, slide out of the smooth leather chair, and end up in some weird position where I showed Lawyer Guy my tiger-striped undies.

But no sooner had I bent over than darkness claimed me.

Hey! I'm Kristi. I write romances that will tug your heartstrings and laugh out loud mysteries. In all my stories you'll fall in love with the cast of characters, they'll become old, fun friends. **My one hope** is that I create stories that *satisfy any of your book cravings* and take you away from the rut of everyday life (sometimes it's a good rut).

When I'm not writing I'm repurposing Happy Planners or drinking a London Fog (hot tea with frothy milk).

I'm the mom of 2 and a milspouse (retired). We live in the Pacific Northwest and are under-prepared if one of the volcanoes erupts.

Here are 3 things about me:

- I lived on the outskirts of an active volcano (Mt.Etna)
- A spider bit me and it laid eggs in my arm (my kids don't know that story yet)

- I grew up in Central Florida and have skied in lakes with gators.

I'd love to get to know you better. Join my Read & Relax community and then fire off an email and tell me 3 things about you!

Not ready to join? Email me below or follow me at one of the links below. Thanks for popping by!

You can connect with Kristi at any of the following:
www.kristirose.net
kristi@kristirose.net

JOIN KRISTI'S READ AND RELAX SOCIETY

I hope you enjoy this book. I'd love to connect and share more with you. Be a part of my Read & Relax Society and let's get to know each other. There, I'll share all sorts of book information. You're guaranteed to find an escape. You'll also be the first to know about my sales and new releases. You'll have access to giveaways, freebies, and bonus content. Think you might be interested? Give me a try. You can always leave at any time.

If you enjoyed this book I would appreciate if you'd share that with others. I love when my friends pass along a good read. Here's some ways you can help.

Lend it , Recommend it , Review it
XO, Kristi

Made in the USA
Columbia, SC
09 April 2023

15145276R00102